INFORMED SOURCES

Books by Lawrence Kamarck

The Dinosaur
Recipient of the
Edgar Allan Poe Special
Award, 1969

The Bellringer

The Zinsser Implant

INFORMED SOURCES

A Novel by
Lawrence Kamarck

The Dial Press
New York

Published by
The Dial Press
1 Dag Hammarskjold Plaza
New York, New York 10017

Manufactured in the United States of America

First printing

Library of Congress Cataloging in Publication Data

Kamarck, Lawrence.
Informed sources.

I. Title.
PZ4.K1487In   [PS3561.A417]   813'.5'4   79–11049
ISBN 0–8037–4110–3

For all my daughters
and
all my sons

INFORMED SOURCES

CHAPTER ONE

Wes, I'm such a dodo. I really don't understand anything, but I think I do, the letter began without preamble.

As you know, as you must know now, I didn't make the mission. I'm dead, fucking finally really dead. I'm sure Lessy is going around with a shiteating happy grin, pleasure dripping from his fat lips. I know things about him that you wouldn't believe. That's wrong. You'd believe them but you'd accept them. It took seven years of solitary confinement for you to get to a state for the psychiatrists to label you a paranoid schizophrenic. Lessy was that to begin with. For Christ's sake, maybe you were, too. You were a pretty secretive guy at school. I never felt I knew you too well even though we were friends.

I'm sorry I never was able to reach you about Lessy during those months you lived with me after Indochina. He is planning something big. I know it just from what I've seen. I know damn well that MPI is not just another proprietary of the CIA. It's been financing political campaigns, including that of the President. That stuff about it being a cover is just so much shit. I'm distressed that you didn't tell me. For Christ's sake, you run the Goddamn thing for Lessy.

You're right. It doesn't make a hell of a lot of difference now that I'm undoubtedly dead. But it does, because I know Lessy's responsible. It hurts to know that there isn't anyone to stop him from doing any Goddamn thing he wants. That's a hell of a reason for living, isn't it? (I had another one. I'll get to that.)

If you get into any trouble whatsoever, I want you to know that I've been in contact with a senator and he knows what I know. He may try to get you to testify. Jesus, trust him. Even as I write the word "trust," I realize you won't. I know you never trusted me, but thank God, you never trusted Lessy either. Listen, try it once. Just this once. Only don't let it be Lessy you try it with. The son of a bitch now controls every official undercover and federal police force in the country, and more. There's no one to stop him if he wants to run it all. Christ, you know this already and it doesn't scare you.

Perhaps I reached you and you might have a soft spot for me or might at least be curious about whether Lessy planned my death. I can't be certain, but it feels like a fucking Lessy trap out there. If this is true, remember what I once told you about Kulbers and the Farbie Institute. This is Lessy's one weakness and he doesn't even know it.

I had another reason for wanting to stay alive. I can't think of a better person to entrust with it because I need one favor from you and I know you'll do it for me. You'll be perfect because you don't get emotionally involved.

I've never told anyone and it's not in my records, but I have a daughter. Before I went to Yale, I had a girl friend. I'm sure you wouldn't be interested in the details. Anyway, we had a baby girl (obviously not an infant anymore). I've been suffering inside ever since. I love that kid. I have seen her only at a distance, but she sits in my heart.

Over the years I've taken care of the harsher parts of her life. I arranged for scholarships so she could get a good education, medical care, money, private lessons. The man she thinks of as her father is a bumbling nice-guy who never made enough to do more than survive. Me, I even had a private detective check on her every now and then, just to make sure no one was taking advantage. (He scared off two teenage creeps during her adolescent crazy years.)

More recently I arranged an associate's position with a Washington law firm for her after she graduated from Columbia Law School. To be perfectly honest, I thought I might like to see her more frequently. After only a year, she apparently decided to open her own office. I don't think she understands what sort of world we live in here. My taking care of her needs has made her an innocent. It frightens me to think of what I've done.

I know this whole business is foreign to you, but I'm asking you to watch over her. Maybe you can correct what I've done and give her some sense of the reality of this godforsaken world. Please, please, as a favor for a friend.

I trust you, Wes, more than any other person I know. Perhaps it's because we've known each other for so long. Perhaps it's because I've never found in you those rules the rest of us have by which we make judgments about other people's behavior. I've never heard you criticize anyone's action, no matter how bizarre.

You always know the game. Teach my daughter, Please.

Her name is Marvina Peters. (Her father-of-record is a Marvin. I suppose her mother intended to call her Junior if she had been a boy in order to elicit Marvin's sense of responsibility. Nothing I could do about that.) She's in the phone book.

Thanks. I know you'll do this for me.

Owen Fuller

Wes Carpenter was not even thoughtful after reading the letter from his friend. Crumpling the envelope, he tore each page into small pieces, and stuffed everything in a pocket.

The woman on the bed grinned at him. "You're a hot shit," she said. "The first letter that's come for you since I've known you and you don't show any emotion. You tear the thing up."

"Where's the envelope?" he asked. "The envelope addressed to you that held my letter?"

She pointed to a wastebasket in the corner of the shabby room.

"Get it."

"I don't know what it is with you." She squinted.

"Get it, Liz," he repeated.

She reluctantly heaved herself from the lumpy bed and padded to the corner in her bare feet, pawed through the debris and pulled out an envelope. Turning, she handed it to him.

He took it and mashed it into the same pocket he had put the other material.

"Jesus," she said, "I hope you don't make it a habit."

He stared at the naked woman getting back into bed. "Habit?"

"That's a joke. That's the first letter I ever got for you. I almost forgot what you said way back about letters maybe coming for you here."

"You won't ever get one again. I don't have anyone else to write to me."

"Won't this guy write you again?"

"No," he said. "He won't write again."

"You going to stay around long enough to drop your pants? Or is this it?"

"This will be all for today." He tugged out his wallet and found a hundred dollar bill.

"You're not very sexy," she grumbled.

He placed the bill at the foot of the bed. "Not today. I have too much on my mind."

"Will I see you next week?"

"I don't think so. It might be some months before I return. I have something to do that will require some time."

"You want me to come up to your place?"

"No."

"It won't be any trouble," she said, tilting her head in a seductive fashion.

"No."

"You got some freebie stuff?"

"No. I couldn't possibly afford it." He smiled. "I'll be back."

"I'll wait for you, baby."

The limousine picked him up, as scheduled, on O Street at a quarter of one. No words were exchanged with the driver. Troubled by Owen Fuller's letter, Carpenter sat stiffly during the ten minutes it took to drive to the garage below MPI headquarters. The only thought that went through his mind was *What the hell do you do with a young woman who's stupid enough to open a law office in Washington?*

In the dark parking lot he leaped from the limousine directly into the private elevator. The white-haired operator bowed his head and closed the door. A moment later the door reopened on a gleaming white corridor. He plunged from the elevator and rushed down the hall, through his secretary's empty office and into his own. It was a massive room dominated by a large oak desk in the middle. Heavy wine-colored drapes were pulled across each window. He stood just inside the door and searched the room, staring suspiciously at the corners of the dim interior, his eyes slowly scanning the walls, the ceiling, and finally the desk, its ornate lamp, and the beige telephone. Deciding that everything was in order, he closed the door behind him and locked it.

Wes wondered if Fuller's daughter understood anything about Washington—how dangerous it was, how careful one had to be, in order to live and stay alive. One had to distrust everyone and everything. It had always been that way, though he knew that he had been aware of it before most of those around him.

Walking back around his desk, he suddenly crouched

down and crawled into the kneehole, bunching up his skinny legs, wrapping his arms around his knees, his head resting between them.

"Well, what now?" he asked aloud, his voice normal and clear, yet little more than an indistinct mumble escaped beyond his cramped space. "Goddamn Fuller, I kept telling him to keep his mouth shut, didn't I? The important thing was to stay alive. It's always been that." He remembered Fuller at school: content and proud, a midwestern kid at an eastern college who had never been aware that it was hard to stay alive. Comparing the way he himself was at that time, he knew that his own childhood had had at least the benefit of being a reflection of reality. He recalled his father suddenly striking out, catching him off guard, knocking him down, screaming an obscenity. It was important to be careful then, even at night, when that angry son of a bitch howled drunkenly, slamming his fists against walls and shouting against life. Carpenter knew that Owen Fuller had never had to booby trap the floor of his room with sharp objects at night so that he would have warning of his father. The loneliness of those years wasn't bad; it got him into Yale, what with his incessant study, then through the years in Cambodia.

"You told Owen that but it didn't help. He wouldn't listen. If he had, he could have taken care of his own daughter. You told him to get out from under Lessy, but he wouldn't listen to you.

"He was your friend.

"I don't have friends.

"Fuller was. What are you going to do about it?

"The son of a bitch. The son of a bitch wouldn't listen. I'll get even for him. But no more than that. I'll find out if Lessy's to blame. That's the least I can do."

CHAPTER TWO

He had a feeling of exultation. The explosions, like fireworks, flashed inside his head. The wire fencing had gone first and then the side of the building, and then the Farbie Building was a gaping shell loaded with people milling around him as he moved resolutely among them. He was pleased; no one seemed to be injured, only panicked by the noise, the suddenness of the smoke, the plaster dust, the continuing blasts on the outside, the public announcement system screaming for calm and abandonment of the building. It had taken forty-five seconds to open everything and to be inside.

Carpenter wanted the Akerman office, the Study Group Analysis Section on Historical Operational Directives. As he made his way toward the center of the building, he tossed charges into offices vacated by fleeing workers. The explosions made the hallways total chaos, no one knowing in what direction to move. There was screaming when the lights went out. It would be a long time before the Farbie Institute would be able to conduct further commissioned studies. He switched on his flashlight.

The door of the Akerman office was locked and secure. He stepped back and tossed a charge at the wall, and it collapsed.

The alarm siren was a piercing wail competing with the shrieks of people and falling materials as the building began to break apart. He stuffed his pockets with the microfilm disks from the desk containers, set a final charge, and left, joining the general melee to the exit.

The charge went off as he entered the main hall. He walked out with the crowd.

He glanced at his watch. It had taken two minutes, fortyfour seconds. When he reached the grassy knoll above the building, he looked back to discover that fires had broken out. He stood silent, ecstatic, wanting to scream out. He had done it!

What a great job! I blew the fucking thing up! I did it!

Below, vehicles began arriving, fire trucks, police cars. Men in uniforms were scurrying among those pouring out of the building, shouting and shoving, organizing the chaos. Clouds of black smoke suddenly broke through the roof followed by flame.

The tension was still with him when he left. Coiled internally as he was from the excitement, his face—yellowish after years of quinine, atabrine, and chloroquine that he took for malaria—was heavily lined as though marked with an eyebrow pencil. Ruts plowed from his mouth and eyes, furrows crossed his brow.

In the photographic studio set up in the basement of his town house, he ran an enlargement of one of the microfilms taken from the Farbie Building—a long memorandum from Roland Lessy to the director. He pressed the timer and a light flashed briefly in the darkroom. There was still a night of work ahead. He smiled. There was another memo after this one. Both had to be distributed to columnists and a broad assortment of congressmen.

He remembered his original acceptance of Lessy's words:

"I'm not going to let one of you bastards get away with embarrassing our government if you're caught. The Goddamn game is to eliminate yourself if you're so fucking incompetent as to get caught. We're not going to have another Francis Gary Powers. That's not how the game is played and you better fucking understand it. And you got nothing to kick about. All you bastards make enough money, the place is loaded with all the tail you can handle. And if you're good and make it, you'll have a contented old age doing any fucking thing you want. But make a mistake and that's it. If you don't follow orders, that's it."

He glanced down at the photograph wet with chemicals.

It concerns me that the mood of the country does not seem to support the moral standard in espionage that no agent be taken alive. I perceive this as having an influence among agents in the field. I intend to correct this.

In the darkness Carpenter paused and sought the image of Lessy's gray corpulent face. Fleetingly he caught it. "You son of a bitch," he said aloud as he read.

I've decided to use Fuller as an example. He's a bad influence here, raising unnecessary ethical questions. Because of this he'll be ideal, providing the necessary heroic example of the man who sacrifices himself for the security of our nation. I've made all the arrangements.

CHAPTER THREE

Carpenter jumped from the limousine before it had completely stopped and hurried to the door between the two shops. Marvina Peters's office was off Pennsylvania Avenue SE in a small two-story building over a barber shop and drugstore. He stepped inside, turning to study the busy street. Satisfied that no one had seemed to pay attention to him, he darted up the narrow flight of stairs, two steps at a time.

It was gloomy. A dim bare bulb lit the landing. He hesitated, looking down both ends of the hall. It was empty, all doors were closed. He edged along the corridor and quickly entered the last door on the left.

A skinny woman with gray disorderly hair glanced up at him, not at all surprised at his sudden dramatic entrance.

"You may go right in," she said.

"Thanks." He went into the room beyond her.

Marvina Peters stood up. A slim woman in her middle twenties, she had long black hair that curled around her ears and spread over the collar of a gray mannish summer jacket. Her blue eyes glistened. She seemed puzzled.

"I hope you're not nervous about tomorrow," he said.

"You must be Mr. Carpenter. Wesley Carpenter?"

He gave her time to study him before nodding. Sitting, stretching his legs out in front of him, he said, "I suppose you have deposited the money I sent you."

"You want it back?" She seemed worried. "As a matter of fact, I didn't expect that much. Twenty thousand is a lot of retainer."

"I just wanted to know that you banked it. It's not much but it's safer in a bank." Fuller was right, he decided. She would need help in Washington, she shouldn't be in Washington. "You seem nervous," he said.

"I tried to be honest with you when you called. I don't know about you or why you're testifying before a Senate committee. You weren't helpful. All I know is what I read in the newspapers."

"That's not much. Did it worry you?"

"I couldn't see how I could help you. You do know that I'm just trying to get started? I thought you might have made a mistake."

"No mistake."

"You're sure?"

"Positive."

She still didn't seem to feel any relief from uncertainty. "I don't know what I can do for you. It's all very mysterious."

"Relax. You don't have to know anything."

"It's more mysterious than you know. I just received a call from a presidential assistant about you."

"That doesn't surprise me." It did surprise him momentarily. "What did he want?"

She paused. "Whether I was going to see you today."

Now there was no surprise whatever. "That was Sy Basset. That's a stupid question. Only Basset would have asked. There must have been something else going on. He knows damn well I was coming here. He has my office bugged and gets daily reports from my secretary."

"You're not serious."

He was confused. Serious? Of course he was serious. His eyes became slits as he watched her face. She didn't know anything about Washington. She knew nothing. "It happens to everybody," he said. He wondered if it would help her to understand that even her secretary was on more than one payroll.

"Should you be telling me?"

"You're new to this," he said. "You should know what to expect." Fuller was right about his daughter: she was an innocent. "What else did Basset want?"

"He wanted me to go to a telephone booth and call him back. I told you it was exotic."

"When?" he asked.

"Later. He told me where and when."

He became thoughtful. It didn't make sense. It was conceivable that Basset might have wanted her to use another phone, a public phone, to tell her something he wouldn't discuss on her own line, or to tell her where to pick up a drop of information or money. Neither was logical, however. "You're sure it wasn't somebody else who called you?" he asked.

"It was Basset."

"Don't phone. Trust me. There's an old adage I follow: If it doesn't make sense, don't do it."

"If I followed your rule, I wouldn't be talking to you."

He watched her lips tighten and her eyes narrow, her face showing determination.

"Don't worry," she said. "I'll tell you tomorrow what it was all about. You can trust me."

Trust? He smiled. For the moment he'd leave it at that. "How about tomorrow?"

"I was asked to have you there at two tomorrow afternoon."

"I thought Kulbers would be done today."

"The committee counsel told me that he'd be finished tomorrow morning. He seems to hold great faith in your appearance. I gather that Kulbers was a big disappointment and has been pretty dull. The counsel is very hopeful about you. Though he seemed troubled when I told him that I had never met you and was going to see you for the first time today."

"I bet that bothered him."

"I felt inadequate. He kept mentioning Roland Lessy. I didn't understand. I thought Lessy was said to have left the country after those memorandums were published."

"Don't worry about it. If they don't like dull witnesses, they won't like me. I'll be dull as hell." He hoped that would end the discussion. "It shouldn't take long. There's nothing I can tell them."

"The counsel seems to think you have a lot to tell them."

"Believe me, you don't have any worries." He was speaking too sharply, he decided. Too quickly. He sensed that he was arousing her interest rather than dulling it. Her eyes disturbed him; they were too blue, too alert, too much like Fuller's. "There's nothing for you to do," he said. "The less you know, the better." He stood and began to leave.

"What's the fuss about if you're going to be so dull?"

"There'll be no fuss."

"I suppose you're entitled to keep me completely in the dark. I suppose there's nothing I can do about that. You've paid me enough money to do what you want, but I don't feel right about it. I've seen enough about you in various columns to be uneasy."

He watched her eyes and felt them.

"You know, Mr. Carpenter, that there have been items printed about you that suggest you're responsible for destroying the Farbie Building and disturbing the material on Owen Fuller," she said.

"It doesn't concern me what's said."

"Were you Fuller's best friend?"

"Where did you pick that up?" He cautioned himself about his reaction. He had to be more deliberate—calm.

He smiled. "Someone's guessing. I was a spook, young lady. No one knows anything about me. For a good part of my life, I was one of Lessy's boys in Clandestine Services. No one touches me unless Lessy says so. Certainly the Senate doesn't. He owns the Senate."

She didn't continue. She stared without comprehension, not focusing on him or anything in the small shabby room.

He had told her too much. She was startled, trying to absorb information beyond her ability to understand. In the silence that filled the office as if silence were something loud, he knew that the conversation was over. He wondered why he had a sudden pang of guilt, an odd desire to reach across the desk and pat her head, to repeat once again that everything would be all right. He was almost moved to tears as he studied her. He tore his eyes from her pale face and looked out the office window behind her, seeing the building across the street and the hazy sky beyond. No one was innocent, not even Fuller's daughter. He glanced quickly back at her face and wondered if that was true. It gave him an uneasy feeling to experience guilt.

"Why do you need me?" she asked, her voice uncertain.

"Maybe I'll tell you some day."

"Not now?"

"Not now." The guilt had converted to a sense of shame; that also was new. "I'll see you tomorrow," he said, and turned toward the door, ripping himself from the new emotion, hoping that it would abruptly end. It didn't.

As he passed Marvina Peters's drab secretary, he exchanged an envelope, containing a hundred dollar bill, for a slip of paper. On it was the address of the outside public phone from which the lawyer was supposed to make her call to Sy Basset and the time it was to be made.

His limousine pulled up as he exited the building.

"Take me home," he said.

"Yes, sir."

He stared out of the window as they drove through Washington, knowing that he was about to act, yet knowing that he wouldn't be able to describe what he was about to do. He was still disturbed by Fuller's daughter.

Seven blocks from the Capitol the limousine was abreast of his house and slowing. He jumped out, saying, "Thanks," and was at the front door after a quick walk up the path. He closed the door and waited, listening to the stillness. Finally satisfied that the house was sufficiently silent, he ran upstairs and ducked into his bedroom. He took out the slip of paper Peters's secretary had given him. The phone booth was near her office. The time noted was six forty-five.

He tore up the note on the way to the bathroom and dumped the pieces into the toilet. Opening the medicine cabinet, he removed what appeared to be a styptic pencil, unscrewed its cover, and poured a dab of brown grease into his hand. This he spread over his face, neck, and hands until his normally yellowish skin was a shiny gleam of darkness. Staring at himself in the mirror, he rubbed a few light spots near his ears. Then he grinned appreciatively at himself and nodded approval.

Before leaving the second floor, he stopped at the utility closet and swapped his suit coat for a painter's smock speckled with a variety of colors. Hiding his shirt and tie beneath the new covering, buttoning it to the neck, he descended the stairs and left his house by its rear door. He completed his clothing transformation in the small tool shed outside, slipping on a pair of worn dirty blue coveralls, a battered painter's cap, and mud-splattered overshoes.

He reached under a shelf and pulled out a lunch pail. Inside, hidden in its false bottom, was a claylike gray coil. Pinching off a small piece of it, he searched a side shelf and found a book of ordinary paper matches. He stuffed both items inside a pocket, then let himself out the back gate and jauntily walked down the alley between the buildings. He sauntered at first then gradually assumed a shambling step and began to appear tired, as though every move forward were a weary effort. On Pennsylvania Avenue he stopped to wait for the bus. He was a black man heading home from work.

He went directly to the phone booth on the corner, moving resolutely, making no effort to check the area, showing no suspicion. Taking the receiver off its hook and wedging it into a shoulder, he pretended to converse while he took a piece of the sticky coil from his pocket and squashed it along the bottom of the phone box. One end hung down to the ledge. He took the book of matches, folded the cover back, and implanted it carefully in the loose string of clay-like material.

Bending one match from the book, he ignited it with a lighter and left, closing the glass door. Walking briskly along the street, he finally stepped into a storefront.

There was a loud explosion.

He turned to look and watched a phone hurtling straight up while the booth walked up the sidewalk and then suddenly collapsed with a crash of broken glass. Carpenter's face fleetingly brightened, his lips open to a silent laugh, his eyes appreciatively wide and sparkling. He glanced at his watch. Six forty.

A fat man bustled out of the shop, breathless. "What happened?"

"Don't know, boss."

The fat man continued past to the curb. "Jesus," he said as he went, "it's not safe anywhere." There were more people streaming along the sidewalk toward the destroyed booth.

Carpenter saw Marvina Peters across the street. She was

standing rigid, staring at the place where the booth had been. She appeared to be stunned.

Then he noticed the blue Volkswagen bus with two men inside, parked down the street from Marvina. He knew them. They were under contract to the CIA for special personal jobs, those defined by Roland Lessy. It was clear what her call was to accomplish. For some reason she was ticketed for kidnapping. Maybe worse.

There didn't seem to be a ready answer as to why Basset had set it up. Why the hell was the President involved? Had the little bastard taken over Lessy's operation?

He strode across the street to the Volkswagen and leaned into the open window on the driver's side. "I got something to tell you," he said and rolled his eyes. The two men grinned as they pushed toward him to listen.

The two wouldn't be missed, he decided, and it might teach the little bastard a lesson.

He killed the driver first with a sharp blow at the bridge of his nose. The other looked surprised and still had the remains of his grin as Carpenter slammed a fist across his Adam's apple.

He looked around him as he withdrew from the window. No one had noticed.

CHAPTER FOUR

He woke up feeling stiff and suddenly remembered that he was still in the closet, though he hadn't meant to fall asleep. "The bastard's getting to me," he said. Opening the door, he saw it was early morning, a smear of gray light entering the windows. His bed and bureau were black shadows.

As he uncoiled, he felt pain course down his back and legs. He waited until it subsided before moving again. Suddenly he was chilled, as if plunged into a cold ocean. "Damn it," he said and moved swiftly to the bedstand and found his bottle of quinine. "What a lousy time for an attack!" He took one pill and put on the bathrobe bunched at the foot of the platform bed.

He sat on the side of the bed, turned the light on, plugged in the phone, and dialed his office.

"Yes?"

"This is Carpenter. Any calls?"

"Two. One from Marvina Peters. The other from Sy Basset."

"Nothing from the President?"

"Just the two."

"Thanks." He hung up. He was beginning to feel warm, as if the room were an oven. Sweat beaded on his forehead. Putting his hands behind him for support for a moment, he lurched forward and pulled off his bathrobe and the top of his pajamas. Then he fell back and closed his eyes. He wondered if he was going to throw up. He decided that he didn't care.

It was a dizzying ride down. He always hated parachute jumping; it was unreal, falling without really falling, knowing that something was holding him back, as if some god were lowering him to the ground. He felt sick. He felt he was going to vomit on all that nice greenery below. He didn't. He listened to the air as it rushed past him into the snapping canopy above him. He pulled on one set of guides and floated at a quickened pace toward a blackened burn area.

"Oh, dear Christ!" he yelled as he hit. The ground was littered with stubs of wood, shards of sharp metal, rocks, and pointed stakes sticking up at him. "Bastards! Fucking bastards!" He wiggled as he was dragged over rocks and metal, falling on his back, hooking a foot in one of the stakes, slicing wildly with his hands as he tried to slip from his chute. "You sons of bitches!" he screamed. Finally he was free. He stayed on his back for a moment, contemplating three more chutes falling far off, their weighty packages slung underneath, looking like coffins.

He turned over on his stomach and looked to the edge of jungle. Nothing of interest, no visible humans. He sat up and unhitched his pack. He began to sweat as he felt the heat. Unzipping his coveralls, he felt a moist vapor escape from his body. He put a carbine together and crammed an ammunition load in its belly, then repacked and strapped the load to his back.

It was the insects that bothered him most. He wasn't disturbed about being in the jungle alone; that was being alone anywhere. It was the damn insects, especially the mosquitoes. He tried his repellant, but his sweat washed it off almost immediately.

Suddenly he knew he was being followed. He sensed it more than knew it. He kept moving north; that's where the other chutes had drifted. In small spots the undergrowth was thick and abrasive. He circled these and continued north, walking softly on the thick spongy surfaces where the trees were highest. Monkeys screamed above him. He screeched back at them.

The ground sloped down as the underbrush became a thick luxuriant pliant mass that fought his every step.

Entangled in his bed covers, he struggled free, wondering if he had been unconscious long. Though his body was damp and his sweat clammy, he was alert. He felt better. His strength would return. He struggled to sit on the side of the bed and took deep breaths, his stomach flattening and then swelling in rapid succession. ("You don't have malaria. It's your body's reaction, a sort of hysteria in response to too much tension," the doctor had said.)

"Bullshit."

He pulled out the drawer in his bedstand and found his address book. After leafing to the right page, he dialed.

"Basset?"

"Yeah. Who's this?" It was a foggy early morning voice.

"Carpenter. You called earlier."

"Jesus Christ, it's four in the morning."

"That's right. I'm returning your call."

"Christ, I called at eleven."

"What do you want?" he snapped.

"Jesus, it's four in the morning. Let me get my mind together. Eleven is a hell of a lot different than four."

"If you don't remember—"

"I remember. I remember. It's just that I want to make sure I have it straight."

"You have notes?"

"Of course I have notes."

"Then read them to me," Carpenter suggested.

"Wait until I find the damn...."

"Are you in bed?"

"What the hell difference does that make?"

"I'm just curious."

"Go to hell. Here we are. You listening?"

"That's why I called you." He felt strong again. The malaria attack was over.

"It's just a question."

"Ask it."

"What do you know about Operation Little Girl?"

"Is that it?"

"I'm told to get an answer from you before you testify."

"I have to think about it."

"Christ, Mr. Carpenter, you are an annoying public servant."

"You want an answer now?"

"Some answer, yes."

"Best I can do is to say that I know a little."

"Is that your answer?" Basset asked curtly.

"That's it."

"That's a damn poor answer."

"It's the best I can do."

"What happens if the committee asks you about it?"

"Operation Little Girl?"

"That's right. What do you tell the Senate committee about it?"

"Tell the little shit that he'll have to wait and see."

"For Christ's sake, Carpenter, stop calling the President a little shit!"

"What do you object to, little or shit?"

"Very funny. Just don't do it."

"Is that an order?"

"How the hell can I give you orders? I'm just giving advice ... as a friend."

"What's that?"

"Friend?"

"Yes."

"I guess you're right, Carpenter. We're not friends."

"If you want to stay alive, you don't have friends."

Carpenter groped for a handkerchief in the top drawer of the night table, found it, and wiped his forehead.

"What's with your lawyer?" Basset asked.

"She's somewhat naive. That's to be expected; she's new to Washington."

"That's not what I mean." He could almost see Basset's sneer.

"You bothered by her being a woman?"

"No. Everybody gets his kicks in his own way. You like kids; you can have them. We just don't get her, not at all. She missed a phone appointment. When I called her later to find out what happened, she seemed to think that I was trying to kill her. Incredible. She even said that the President was trying to kill her."

"What do you mean, missed a phone call?"

"Don't give me that shit. You know damn well I wanted her to go to an outside booth. We wanted to make arrangements for a money drop."

"Wait a minute. A money drop?"

"The President's idea. He wants to pay her."

"For what? The little bastard *takes* money, he doesn't *give* money."

Basset was silent a moment. "I asked you not to do that. He gets very upset every time he hears you on tape. It's getting worse. Believe me, he doesn't like being called—"

"What did the little bastard want to pay Marvina for?"

"*Cut it out!*" Basset screamed into his phone. "He's not a little bastard!"

Carpenter waited until Basset's breathing returned to normal. "I'd still like to know. What does he think he's buying?"

"The President didn't want any of this to cost you."

"I'll pay my own way, thanks. Tell the little bastard that I'm an independent type. And what the hell is the little cunt doing, using Lessy's goons?" He took the receiver from his mouth and ear and stared at it, listening to the distant indecipherable squeaks from the screeching Basset. He hung up.

Then he went back to the closet, closing the door behind him, squatting down on his heels.

"The little fuck," he spat. "He must think I'm stupid. Now, let's analyze what the President's whore means by Operation Little Girl. Remember, you're dealing with a paranoid and a bunch of little paranoids. They see plots and make them up faster than rabbits reproduce.

"We can be fairly certain that the little bastard is trying to get rid of me. I gave an answer that showed I knew something about Little Girl. Suppose, just suppose, there isn't anything called Little Girl. Then the little bastard will know I'm lying. And if it's bait for a trap, he'll know I swallowed it and he'll play me as he wants.

"Then, you must consider that there may be such a thing as Operation Little Girl. That would mean Lessy is behind it. It's a typical Lessy code name. In which case he's out there somewhere, probably using the little bastard. In either case you've got a problem. Better find out."

The phone was ringing, the sound very faint in the closet.

"That's the whore," he said as he opened the door and stood up. He reached the telephone with long strides.

"Carpenter here."

"This is Sy Basset. Why the hell did you hang up?"

"There wasn't anything more to say. You were getting emotional."

"What was that about Lessy?"

"You don't mind if I'm taping this conversation, do you?"

"In your bedroom, this time of the morning?"

"Don't be innocent."

"Are you kidding?"

"I never kid."

The line went dead.

Carpenter smiled and fell back on his bed. He didn't bother to turn the lights out. He just closed his eyes and was asleep, his legs hanging over the edge of the bed.

The following morning, at ten, he opened his front door as his limousine arrived. He strode down the brick path between the hedges, slipped into the rear seat. The chauffeur slammed the door. While the driver circled back to place, Carpenter looked up out the window. Another dead gray sky.

In a few minutes he was in the garage under his building. The limousine circled the interior and stopped alongside his elevator. Its door was open, and the white-haired operator was standing obsequiously to one side.

Every day he negotiated the entire trip to his office without saying a word to anyone. It was the morning game. He had succeeded again. Some days it was difficult; everyone seemed determined to speak to him, and part of the rules was to speak only when spoken to. He smiled, content, and rode up to his office. His door opened, and his secretary was there with his tray.

"Good morning," she said.

"Is it?"

"I think so." The black coffee steaming in its pewter mug, a Danish pastry resting on a gleaming silver plate—both were placed hesitantly on his desk. She paused, as if waiting for a reaction. He nodded finally, and she left, closing the door.

The phone rang.

"Okay," he said into the receiver.

"Okay," the voice on the other end said.

He hung up and touched the hot mug. It was burning. He picked up the bun and took a large bite, chewing it carefully and thoroughly. His mouth was dry and the crumbs in his throat felt coarse, making him cough. Even though the coffee was still too hot, he sipped some quickly.

Alex Sofer opened the door, moved silently, closed it, stood there as if he had appeared magically. A short stubby man with a shining pink-hued bald head, he wore a broad grin as he strode rapidly to the chair by the side of the desk.

"You ought to get something other than a metal mug. It holds the heat too long."

"It'll cool. It always does." Carpenter opened the right-hand top drawer of his desk and removed two pads of paper, handing one to Sofer.

Sofer stared at the pad a moment and then looked up to meet Carpenter's eyes. They both smiled.

He gave Sofer a pencil from the desk receptacle and took one himself. He said, "It looks like a lousy day." He wrote on the pad, *What do you know about Operation Little Girl?*

"I don't think it will rain." Sofer wrote, *Never heard of it. Who's behind it?*

"There's no sign of that. I think you're right." His pencil scratched out, *It sounds like something of Lessy's.*

"The weather can change abruptly. This is a crummy climate." *I thought he was out of it, had taken off.*

"It's done it before." *I don't know. I have a feeling he's still around. But I'm not sure he's behind Little Girl. Will you check this out?*

"If it rains, at least the farmers will be happy." *When do you need?*

Soon. Try to find something by evening.

"Your coffee's getting cold. I better leave you alone." Sofer rose and saw himself out.

Carpenter gathered up the pieces of paper and took them to the small paper shredder on the table in the corner. He switched it on and fed the sheets into it.

Sofer was right; the coffee was cold. He drank it anyway while munching on the rest of his pastry. He wondered what the listener to his conversation thought about his operations. The inane comments about the weather, endless discussions about rain, clouds, sunshine. Time to pick another subject, he decided. It's too damn obvious. Listeners should have caught on by now. Lessy would know. The little bastard might think that a code was being used, but he would have to be an idiot not to know better.

He rose and returned to his paper shredder. Using a dime, he undid the small screws around the edge of the mechanism. He was upset with himself for not noticing previously that the disposal sack was bolted inside. He lifted out the shredder and peered into the basket.

There were the sheets he had fed in a few minutes earlier; they were intact, not even bent. Removing them, he replaced the shredding mechanism, refastening the screws. Back at his desk, he hastily scratched a series of circles on a new piece of paper, some boxes on another. Returning to the shredder, he fed both into it.

He wondered when it had been discovered that all business in his office was handled in writing. He stuffed the notes he and Sofer had made into his pants pockets. Privacy was almost entirely gone; secrecy was impossible. The only secrecy was in your own mind. That's the only place where it could be kept.

He wrote on his pad: *Get me a list of all employees hired during the last six months and the dates of their employment. Why were they hired? What do they do? Stay out of normal channels. I don't want anyone to know that I'm interested.* He buzzed his secretary.

She appeared instantly.

He touched a finger to his lips.

She smiled and nodded, almost as if she were humoring a child.

He handed her his note, and she left with it and the morning tray. She seemed to be brimming with a happy sense of his trust in her. Foolish woman. He knew that the little bastard would have the contents of his note before the afternoon was over. Christ, everybody needed more than one job to get by. Some had three or four.

He dialed Marvina Peters. "All set?" he asked.

"All set?" she repeated with disbelief. "My God, how can I be all set? They're trying to *kill* me. Why didn't you call me back last night?"

"Who's trying to kill you?"

"They're trying to kill me!"

"What happened?"

She paused. "I don't know," she said. "I went to make that phone call to the White House at the pay phone. Just before I got to the booth, it blew up. One more minute and I would have gone with it."

"What blew up?"

"The telephone booth! Don't you understand?"

"Relax. I don't think anyone wants to kill you."

"You could fool me."

"If someone wanted you dead, you'd be dead. You just have to be watchful."

"I thought I could trust the White House."

"Don't trust anyone."

"That include you?" Her voice sounded thoughtful.

He remembered the Volkswagen. "You have to trust me."

"Can I?"

"It's a stupid question," he said impatiently.

"What are you telling me?"

"Trust me."

Carpenter felt jumpy as he and Marvina moved to their seats up front at the witness table. A news photographer was preceding them and he would suddenly turn and shoot, the flashbulb exploding in eye-blinking brilliance. After the third flash Carpenter discovered that his first reaction of anger, the sudden spurts of desire to kill his tormentor, had passed and that he had to struggle against acceptance, a sort of passive weak acquiescence. When the third and fourth bulb went, he began to remember a small room, a cell without windows, without people, only a bright light high in the ceiling behind a mesh of thin metal. The image vanished.

Marvina glared at the huge chamber, the highly polished long tables with their solid chairs, their curved backs looking like slope-shouldered brown skeletons, the rows of audience seats, the microphones, the glistening chandelier. She seemed uneasy as she approached the table, as though she expected it to splinter apart. Fumbling at the lock on her briefcase, she continued to sneak glances. She patted her dress and tugged it over her knees. Pouring herself a glass of water from the carafe on the table, she spilled the contents and watched stricken as the water soaked some of her papers.

Carpenter mopped the loose rivulets with a handkerchief. He touched her arm, saying, "It'll be all right."

She made an effort to smile.

There weren't many in the room. None of the senators had arrived even though it was nearly two thirty. Perhaps there were a dozen people in the audience. The photographer was alone in the press section. Carpenter decided that

Kulbers, with his dry clerklike noncommittal recitations during days of dull testimony, had taken the shine of interest off the hearing, had made the CIA seem more like the operation of a public library. Fine, he thought. He and Lessy were even. Fuller, Owen Fuller, had been paid back. There was just his daughter left but that was a small debt.

His sense of relief ended abruptly. The members of the press began entering. A crowd of them began flowing down the aisle. They jostled one another noisily, stealing individual looks at Carpenter as they went.

"What's going on?" Marvina asked, twisted about, watching.

"I don't know," he answered.

And the press was followed by the public, a flood filling the empty seats, and soon the room was packed.

The senators still hadn't arrived, but the space behind their table also began filling. A hawk-faced man in his fifties brushed by this group and crossed the area in front of Carpenter. He had heavy eyebrows and intense eyes.

"Mr. Carpenter, we've never met. My name is William Roose. I'm majority committee counsel. At the moment I'm the only counsel. I wanted to talk to you before we began. I wanted to tell you that this will be a tricky business. The senator is on your side—Senator Dobentz, that is. He wanted me to tell you that he knew Owen Fuller and knows all about Lessy. Whether you realize it or not, the senator is *grateful* about the Farbie Building and the release of the Fuller-Lessy memorandums.

"It gave us the chance to steamroller this committee into operation. It's still tender business, so hang in there, even if it looks like it might get rough. We've got to do it this way. Lessy has it wrapped up unless we can arouse the public. It may look like we're enemies, but we have to get the truth. We need you to explain about Lessy. Just remember, we're after Lessy, not you. Any questions?"

"I don't know what you're talking about," Carpenter said.

The hawk-faced man moved back and studied Carpenter. His eyebrows hooded in puzzlement. Then he said, "For heaven's sake, man, you've got to understand. Lessy has it set up and is about to take over. We can stop him. With your help, we can stop him. We can't do it without you."

"I still don't know what you're talking about."

"God help us." The committee counsel turned on his heels and went to the head table and sat down. He continued to stare at Carpenter. In his face was disbelief.

Marvina Peters said, "What was that about?"

"You heard me. I don't know. I think he was trying to trap me into something."

"I couldn't tell," she said. "Be careful."

Four senators arrived and took their seats at the front table. One of them, the committee chairman, sitting next to Roose, leaned toward his counsel. The two, their faces taut, looked over at Carpenter as they conversed.

He felt bewildered. Lessy was gone, vanished, humiliated after publication of the Fuller material—lost. Then he remembered Operation Little Girl and the Volkswagen.

It was ten minutes of three.

The committee chairman banged his gavel. "Mr. Wesley Carpenter," he said.

"Yes, sir."

"Would you please stand up?"

The preliminaries began; the swearing to tell the truth; yes, he had counsel with him. Marvina introduced herself and gave her business address.

Two of the four senators were apparently there only to make a quorum of the committee. They looked as if they might leave at a moment's notice and had worried expressions. Sitting at one end of the head table, they whispered to one another and kept their eyes on the chairman. The fourth senator sat facing them from the opposite end, a legal pad in front of him.

"Do you have a statement you'd like to make, Mr. Carpenter?" Committee Counsel Roose seemed hopeful, his tone expectant.

"No, sir."

"None?" Surprise.

"No, sir."

Roose's eyes darted to the chairman, who motioned for him to press on.

"Would you please give us a brief statement about your background?" His eyes were piercing.

Carpenter paused. They were still expecting something; he wondered what. He recited his service record beginning with his recruitment from Yale by the CIA, leaping the years quickly with summations of where he'd spent time: three years in Africa, five in Latin America, approximately seven in the Far East.

"Could you be more specific?"

"No, sir. Considerations of national security forbid me to speak more specifically."

"Surely you can be more specific than Far East."

"I suppose I might call it Indochina."

"Could you give us the years that you spent there?"

"No, sir, for the same reasons."

"Please continue."

"I was appointed, or should I say, requested to form MPI."

"By whom?"

"Roland Lessy."

The counsel smiled. "Please describe MPI."

"It's a loose association of trade organizations throughout the world. As everyone now knows, it became the fundamental cover for agents of the Central Intelligence Agency. Of course, that's no longer true."

"Please explain for the record what you mean."

"Once it was publicly exposed, it became useless for clandestine purposes and is today quite legitimate."

"It does not presently function in the role of an aid to the CIA?"

"That's right."

"What's right?"

"It has nothing to do with the CIA."

Roose looked doubtful. "Nothing?"

"Absolutely nothing."

"Aren't you still an employee of that agency?"

"No, sir, I'm not."

The committee chairman and Roose held a hurried conference, the counsel shaking his head as if denying what he had just heard. The one senator who seemed to have no connection with the other three—sitting alone, showing no anxiety, displaying interest by writing notes—was grinning. It was a flat face with blubbery folds, organized suddenly into a broad curve of thin lips and unnaturally white teeth. What does he find so funny, Carpenter wondered.

"MPI, I take it, is no longer a proprietary corporation," Roose said.

"That's right."

"It once was."

"That's right."

The smiling senator leaned forward. "I object to this line of questioning," he said.

The chairman suddenly looked fearful, his eyes flitting from the senator to Roose. "Perhaps the senator from Idaho could give me some basis for his objection."

The smile grew broader. "I don't like it. I just don't like it."

"That's not exactly a basis."

"It's the only one you need."

The chairman and Roose put their heads together and

began a lively argument. The final sentences could be heard in the chamber. "Damn it, we can't fold now. We still have a chance."

The senators stared at Carpenter.

Roose once again faced his microphone. "When did MPI cease being considered a proprietary by the CIA?"

The senator from Idaho began to laugh, his flap of gray-white hair shaking with each outburst. The folds of facial skin became a smooth surface except for the recurrent laugh wrinkles that appeared as deep commas around his mouth.

Along with the others in the room, Carpenter was held by the sight. What's the son of a bitch laughing about? The last question from Roose was forgotten. Marvina whispered, "What's going on? I don't understand any of this." Carpenter shrugged innocently.

There was giggling in the audience. The three senators, including the chairman, were leaning forward staring wide eyed at the senator from Idaho. They appeared frightened. His laughter echoed through the hall. Suddenly the senator from Idaho stopped and the room fell dead silent.

The committee chairman quickly recovered and, shifting his papers, commented: "I think we can proceed. Yes, I think we should go on. Proprietaries are not really why we're meeting. Also, I don't believe Mr. Carpenter is qualified to answer as to whether the CIA still considers MPI a proprietary or not." He didn't return the angry look from Roose.

Roose finally lowered his eyes to the documents before him, studying them, leafing through them. As he looked up and seemed about to ask a question, the senator from Idaho shouted into his microphone at the witness: *"Don't tell us that!"*

Carpenter was confused. He hadn't said anything. "Don't tell you what, senator?"

"What about the Owen Fuller business and the Farbie Building?"

"What's wrong with him?" Marvina whispered.

"I've read about them, senator, just as you have. Are you making an accusation that I'm involved because of the reports made by several columnists?"

"I've got my sources, well-informed sources."

"I imagine you have. I don't. I sometimes wish I did."

Rest a moment. Look sincere. Look at the other senators and then make an appeal for fairness. Some of them must know that he's either stoned or insane.

"Let's be fair, senator. I'll answer any questions about matters that I know about. I certainly can't when I don't. You wouldn't want me to speculate about reports in the media. I wouldn't classify that as fair."

He relaxed; that ought to do it.

"Are you saying that reports printed about you and the Fuller incident are lies?" The simple face had become squeezed and mean, an angry mask of indignation.

"Are you suggesting that I was personally involved?"

"Answer my question!"

"I'm getting a little old for that sort of activity." Now, this must be carefully worded. "My company was not involved. The reports are lies."

"What about the Farbie Building?" The same intense anger.

"I give you the same answer."

"You weren't connected with that incident?"

"Again you're suggesting that I personally blew it up."

"You hated Roland Lessy, didn't you?"

"No, sir. I respected him and I still do."

"Would you say that it was possible that the memorandums attributed to Roland Lessy about Owen Fuller were fakes, manufactured to discredit Lessy?"

"I don't know."

"Is it possible? That's a simple question!"

"I suppose it's possible."

"You were at Yale with Owen Fuller, weren't you?"

"Yes, sir."

"You were friends?"

"I suppose so."

"Suppose? Come, Mr. Carpenter. You were friends or you were not friends."

"We were friends, yes."

"You lived together after your return from Indochina."

"Briefly."

"Tell us about your time in Indochina. It was in Laos, wasn't it?"

"I'm afraid national security prevents—"

"Don't tell *me* about national security. That's what we're discussing at this moment. National security. It was Laos, right?"

"Cambodia, sir."

"You spent seven years there. It was soon after you joined the CIA. You spent that seven years in a cell. You spent seven years in complete isolation, never once allowed to see another human being. Isn't that right?"

"Yes, sir."

"During those years, you thought only of revenging yourself one day on the man who sent you, Roland Lessy."

"No, sir."

The senator from Idaho paid no attention to the answer as he broke in. "You are skilled in the creation of forgeries?"

Carpenter looked over at the man. "Among other skills."

"I suggest that it was you who wrote those memorandums that now blacken the good name of a most loyal and good public servant, Roland Lessy. You did it from the bitterness of seven long years and the friendship of Owen Fuller."

Carpenter was on his feet. Flashbulbs went off in his

face. (How do they manage to change the bulbs without my seeing them, he wondered. It was a puzzle. He wouldn't sleep; he'd catch them at it one day.) Recovering himself, he sank back to his chair and spent a moment slowly trying to understand just where he was. He tried to remember what had last been said.

The bell rang that called the Senate together for a vote. The committee chairman was quick to suspend the hearing for the day, announcing that it would continue the following morning at ten. The room emptied.

"Are you all right?" Marvina asked, looking pale herself.

He sat watching the front of the room. Everyone of consequence had gone. "He took me, didn't he? The son of a bitch really put me through it. None of it is true."

"You'll have a chance to correct it tomorrow."

Roose emerged from a door behind the senatorial table. He was white, his skin drawn. He approached Carpenter and Marvina warily, as if they were dangerous. "Now you know," he said.

"I'm not sure what I know," Carpenter said.

"You blew up the Farbie Building. That doesn't concern us. We can't fight Lessy unless you open up on him. We're not after you, Carpenter. But we need to have you admit to everything. It's our only way to get at Lessy."

Carpenter shook his head.

"It's not over yet. We can turn it around tomorrow. I'm not sure we'll have that chance." He bit his lip. "I'm not leaving the Capitol building tonight. I came out here to suggest you do the same, both of you. Your testimony was exactly what they wanted from you. I don't think they want to chance what you might say tomorrow." His eyes went to Marvina. "You're a lucky young lady."

"Why? I don't feel lucky."

"My informant says that you weren't going to be here today."

"They couldn't stop me."

"My dear Miss Peters, the two men who were to prevent you were discovered this afternoon in a Volkswagen, both quite dead." He studied Carpenter. "Perhaps it wasn't all luck. In any case, I suggest that you stay here with me tonight. This building is temporarily a safe haven. I say temporarily because I've been told a new security force is arriving tomorrow to complement the old. However, in the meantime I can find a place for you here. It won't be entirely comfortable but it'll be safe."

"I don't think so," Carpenter said. "I'm not worried."

"Have it your own way. I thought I'd warn you." Roose stared at him for a moment. "I don't think you understand."

"Thanks for the warning. We'll see you." Carpenter took Marvina by the elbow and they left.

"What did he mean?" Marvina asked as they walked along the corridor.

"Don't worry about it. I don't trust him."

CHAPTER FIVE

He looked over at her, the bright young face shining with sincerity. Beyond the face was a semirural back road with fences and gray-green trees and a few neat houses set on sloping fields. The view through the car window changed rapidly as the limousine sped southward through Virginia. She had begun several times, since they'd entered the car, to discuss the hearing. Each time he had stopped her. His attention was on the chauffeur and the locked bulletproof glass drawn between the front and back seats.

They had zipped so quickly through Washington streets and onto the highway that he had admired the driver's ability to avoid stops and slow traffic. He displayed good control. Carpenter wondered how good the driver was beyond that.

"The senator from Idaho," she began again.

He'd let her talk, he decided.

"He acted as if it was his committee."

"In a way it probably was."

"I wasn't any help. I didn't understand."

"I need someone with me. It'll be all right," he said. He heard a faint click and saw the driver's head move slightly.

"I don't know anything."

"I know," he said. "The first thing you must realize is that we can't talk here. There's always someone listening and recording everything we say."

"That's against the law."

He smiled faintly. "That depends on who controls the laws."

Carpenter sat staring at the back of the driver's head, paying little attention as Marvina made a heated denial. He recognized the patter—"This is a nation of laws."—and thought of her father, Owen Fuller. He wondered what it was that made humans quest after taintlessness when surviving was a tainted act. To survive was to well up with guilt for having done so, to feel dirty and unworthy. Perhaps he was insane—as Fuller had always told him—in feeling pleasure only in continuing to live. It's not enough, Fuller had argued. Perhaps that was right; for years now there had been no pleasure, just moments when pain had abated and he could see clearly that he would survive a little longer. There was a kind of joy in that.

"Why aren't you listening to me?" she asked, a helpless quality in her voice.

He turned his head and studied her. "It's a fine lecture," he said. "I think it's a good one for the person who's taping this conversation." Smiling, he added, "I hope the little bastard hears it."

"The little bastard?"

"The President. The listener."

"Oh." She looked fearful and shrank away.

As the limousine headed into the hills, the trees became more plentiful and the farms and little houses fewer. There was a dip ahead where a small lake rested gray and quiet, darker than the sky above. He thumped on the window. The driver turned. Carpenter pointed to the lake.

"Can we stop here?" he shouted. The driver looked at the lake ahead. He seemed momentarily doubtful, but then he grinned and nodded.

"What's here?" Marvina asked.

"We're going to take a walk. It's a nice day for a walk."

He noted the apprehension on her face and said, "It'll be safe. I think of you as a daughter. I've never had a daughter before."

Her fears didn't seem to diminish though, yet he could think of nothing else to say. At least, he thought, she had the normal paranoid emotions most women had about male designs. Fuller hadn't succeeded in keeping her completely innocent.

When the car stopped, he stepped out and walked down to the water's edge. He was a few paces toward the lake when he finally heard the car door slam and heard her footfalls. He stooped to pick up a flat rock, then sent it skipping across the dead water as he waited for her to catch up.

"I finally figured it out," she said coming alongside.

"I thought you would."

"You want to say something and not have it recorded."

"Something like that. That's a good beginning."

"Beginning? I don't understand what that means."

He ignored her question and began to move along the shoreline, conscious that she was following, hearing her soft steps.

"Where are we going?"

"Along the lake and into the trees," he said. "As long as we can be seen, we have a problem."

"My God!" she exclaimed. "I think you're overdoing it."

Not until he had climbed into the grove, and sat down on a mat of dry pine needles, did he look at her. She stood some feet below him, unmoving, still apprehensive, apparently prepared to leave quickly.

"It's safe now," he said.

"You don't trust him? Why don't you find a driver you do trust?"

"Why would I trust a replacement? This way I don't

waste my time being disappointed. It's a matter of prob-
abilities. The chances are that he shouldn't be trusted.
Therefore, I don't."

"That's crazy."

"I don't think it's so crazy. If I were you, I would move
up here out of sight. I think you make a splendid target
where you are."

"You're kidding."

"No. I'm not. At this moment my driver is receiving instructions on how to dispose of us. I don't think you noticed
how startled he was when I asked to be let off here. It's a
perfect setting for his purposes."

As if she finally understood, she moved suddenly from
the openness near the lake to the cover of the grove.

"Very good," he said.

She looked down at him. "Why are you sitting there?
Shouldn't we get out of here?"

"There's no hurry, not at the moment. There really isn't
any escape. This small piece of wood is a hiding place.
There's easily a hundred yards of open field to cross before
we find more cover. He'd pick us off easily if we tried it. Sit
down."

"I can't believe this is happening to me."

"Sit down, damn it!"

She collapsed to the ground.

"I'm sorry about this," he said.

"Why do they want to kill me?" she said quietly.

"You're part of the package. Or maybe you're not. To be
honest . . . I don't really know."

"Is it wise to just sit here?"

"We have to. There's no place to go at the moment. As
long as it looks as if we're no great problem, we're okay."

"You don't seem worried."

"I'm always worried. I don't remember ever being not
worried."

"Then we're going to die." The whites of her eyes shone with barely controlled fear.

"I hope not," he said.

"What does that mean?"

"It means I'm hopeful." He rose from the ground. "I want you to stay where you are and not move. Save your energy as much as you can. You may need it." He removed his jacket, appearing relaxed as he walked farther into the stand of trees. Perhaps she didn't really understand the nature of their predicament; but then death was often a romantic concept for the young and not understood in its finality. But that was good, too. She would hold together as long as it remained a game and viewed the threat of death as an inconvenient personal insult.

There was very little cover within the collection of pines. Most of the wood was matted with brown needles. There were some low bushes in the deep shade of the tall trees and, in a few areas, thick clusters of foot-high weedy plants. At the top he peered out across a field toward the car.

The driver, a pair of binoculars hanging from a strap around his neck, was assembling a rifle. Beside him, resting on the hood of the limousine, was some sort of pistol, outfitted with an auxiliary silencer. Carpenter judged that the driver was fifty yards away.

One way or the other, it would be over in about fifteen minutes. He felt contempt for the driver's smug certainty that it would be a simple matter. Nothing was simple. There had been a mistake made already: he and the girl had been allowed momentary freedom. He smiled and ripped out the linings of his jacket's sleeves and shredded the material into a dozen pieces of flimsy cloth. Then he gathered an equal number of branches, stripping each of its remaining foliage. Tying the long pieces of material to the tops, he stuck the branches into the earth along the edge of the wood, forming a line of blue silk pennants standing four feet high. He did the same with the handkerchief in his pocket, tied the strips to shorter twigs, the tallest perhaps three feet, then pressed them into the soft forest floor.

He returned to Marvina.

"Have you—?" she started to ask.

"Do you have anything red on you—a piece of cloth? We don't have much time. Quickly!"

She slipped off her belt and soon he had a series of red-topped sticks embedded in the ground, small foot-high stubs that led to a small sun-drenched clearing among the trees.

"What the *hell* are you doing?" she asked.

"I'll explain later. For now, just call it magic. Now I want you to strip and lie down in the clearing."

"You're kidding!" She looked at him as if he were crazy.

"We haven't the time. He should be almost here."

"He'll see me!"

"I hope so. If he does, he won't see anything else. Please don't argue. There isn't time."

"For Christ's sake! At least I'm going to die with dignity. I'm sure not going to go naked!"

"That's not the choice. Keep standing there like that and you will surely die." He left her and retreated to the under-side of the wood and halted behind the thickest tree he found. He glanced back at her and saw her undress. The timing was good, he thought, and he turned toward the area where he had placed the highest flags.

He saw a dark form hesitantly moving forward in sudden bursts of activity followed by pauses. The driver was moving cautiously, obviously confused by the attention-getting markers. The man withdrew a few steps. Carpenter thought for a moment that they might have frightened him away, but then the driver began pushing ahead again.

Carpenter could see him clearly now, the head swinging and studying the stakes, his eyes darting beyond them and back, puzzling over them, trying to ignore them, drawn to them again. He was still some forty feet away. There had to be fewer than twenty, and the driver had to be taken at the same moment he saw the naked figure.

It was becoming the magic act, the driver concentrating more on the pennants, his head bent downward as he entered the area of the red strips of cloth. He was less than twenty feet away. Soon.

The driver would see Marvina in two more steps; his eyes played along the stakes ahead as he walked cautiously forward. The hesitancy was gone.

Carpenter estimated that he had less than ten feet to cross to reach the driver. He slipped in back of him. Marvina should be in sight. The soft scuffling steps would stop momentarily. There would be a pause to study the nude form. A momentary suspicion. A quick investigation to see if it was a trap. A sudden realization that Carpenter might have left a decoy so that he might escape. A lunge forward to shoot the girl. Now.

Carpenter caught him as he was raising the pistol to fire. He hit him with his knee in the small of the back and pulled his neck sharply until the head touched his spine and there was a crack of bone. He released him, and the body fell limp and awkwardly to the ground.

"You can get dressed now," he called to the woman in the clearing.

CHAPTER SIX

"Where are we going?" she asked.

He didn't answer her immediately. He kept his eyes on the road, barely conscious of her as she tugged and straightened her clothing. "They're not going to take it away from me," he finally said.

"Take what?"

"Anything."

"Who are they?"

"I'm not sure. I thought it was the little bastard and his people. I'm not sure. There may be others."

"*Who?*"

"The President."

She turned toward him.

"You're not serious."

"It's one possibility."

"It's crazy."

"Maybe, but it's a possibility."

"Why?"

"There are lots of reasons."

"But why me?"

"I don't know. Because you're with me is one answer. They may think you're a threat to them is another." (Maybe they knew she was Fuller's daughter.) "Maybe the guy at the hearing is right."

"Roose?"

"Roose."

"I'm not a threat to anyone."

Had her father's letter been intercepted? "It's not necessarily nonsense," he said.

"I think that's crazy!"

"Perhaps it is, but you're in the nation's capital. Everything's crazy here."

"Is that where we're going?" she asked.

"Washington?"

"Yes."

"We might as well. I have an appointment tomorrow at the Senate. It's a good idea to keep appointments. Roland Lessy disappeared just before he was to testify. It didn't do his reputation any good. Maybe . . ." He hesitated, his eyes fixed on the road. Lessy? Finally he said, "I'm not sure of anything in this."

She fell silent. After a while she said, "I want to stay alive."

"With any luck," he replied, "we'll both make it." As he stared ahead at the roadway, the daylight began to fade and the grayness of the sky slowly blackened. The headlights reached out and seemed to be fingering the center and edges of the dark distance.

"I've never really experienced anyone dying," she said. "My parents are still alive and so are their parents. It's very frightening. I never thought about dying before."

He let her continue to think about it and spent his time concentrating on driving. Having had a driver for so long, he found the task absorbing. The sky above Washington was lit up, a hazy glowing globe, seeming almost gelatinous. He stopped in Alexandria at an outdoor phone booth. After he completed dialing he watched Marvina. Her face was rigid as she stared back unquestioning.

"Alex," he said to the voice that answered, "in about five

minutes I'm going to drive by. I'll pick you up at the corner."

"How about ten?" Alex Sofer asked.

"I can't trust anybody with ten minutes. Too much planning can be done. I've already been careless today. I can't afford two mistakes in the same afternoon."

"The corner in five," said Sofer.

Carpenter glanced at his watch and hung up.

"You'll be all right," he told her when he returned to the car.

Her head swung toward him. "It's beginning to sink in," she said. "Someone was really trying to kill me."

"You knew that." He turned the ignition key.

"I knew it, but I didn't understand it."

"Well, you learned something."

"I don't know what I learned."

"Maybe you will yet." He looked at his watch. "Time to go."

He maneuvered the limousine down a series of narrow streets that ran along the edge of Alexandria and passed the apartment complex where Sofer had his bachelor quarters. A half block from the entrance he parked and switched off the lights and the motor.

"We have a few minutes," he told Marvina. He lifted the pistol he had taken from the driver and handed it to her. "Take this and move into the back seat. Be careful of it. I've taken the safety off and all you have to do is pull the trigger. Very soon we'll have a passenger sitting where you are now. He's a friend, but friends are only as trustworthy as the amount of influence you have over them. I don't think we'll have any problem. If we do, kill him."

"*Kill* him? Just like that: kill him."

"Just like that. Now move to the back seat. He's coming."

She studied the pistol in her hand. He unlocked and opened the sliding glass between front and rear. She left the passenger seat's door open as she shifted to the back seat.

Sofer showed no surprise at this maneuver as he approached. He simply glanced in the back window and slid in next to Carpenter. His bald head was highlighted by the streetlamp. He slammed the door shut and leaned back.

"The driver wasn't trustworthy," Carpenter said.

"Nobody is," Sofer replied.

"Doing anything this evening?"

"Not until now."

"Good." He started up and pulled out of his parking spot. He turned the vehicle around, not going to the corner where he had said he would meet Sofer. "I don't want to take the chance that anyone was listening to my call. It's been a lousy day."

"The driver?"

"He was an amateur. I'm always surprised that anybody depends on amateurs."

"Thank God for amateurs. I love 'em." Sofer laughed at his own joke.

Carpenter didn't speak again until they had left the Alexandria area and were on the main road to Washington. "What did you find out?" he said.

"It doesn't make sense."

"It might to me."

"You want me to talk now?"

"Is it about her?" Carpenter gestured toward the back seat with a thumb.

"If she's Marvina Peters."

Carpenter nodded.

"There's an order out on her. I can't find out who put it in. It was in the iffy category."

"Still?"

"No. It became definite this afternoon. Your chauffeur was told to include her while he was taking care of you. Ap-

parently there was a presidential order." Sofer suddenly
laughed.

"What's funny?"

"It's the ultimate bureaucratic mess."

"What happened?"

Sofer rubbed his eyes. "The White House asked the
Agency for information on her and got a printout response
that she was Operation Little Girl, set up by Roland Lessy,
that she was dangerous."

From the back seat Marvina gasped. "Oh, my God!"

Sofer glanced at her. "That's what was said. Sorry.
Maybe that's not funny. I guess it isn't. Anyway, it was
decided to make you the priority kill."

His eyes never leaving the highway, Carpenter said,
"That's the way the little bastard thinks. It's always a matter of priorities. Anything else?"

Sofer looked down at his hands and seemed lost in
thought for a moment. Then he said, "Nothing much. Lessy
seems to have been involved. It was his idea to do a study
of Marvina Peters. That was right after the Farbie Building
was blown. It also included a prostitute named Liz something. There was another set of reports, but they seemed to
have disappeared when Lessy did. My girl at the Agency
doesn't know if they were filed before or after the explosion
at Farbie."

"What about Lessy?" Carpenter asked. "Any word or
guess about what happened to him?"

"Nothing. Nobody seems to know. No one has replaced
him yet. It's almost as if they expect him to come back."

"Who's operating Clandestine?"

"His assistant."

"Roger Meul?"

"He's still there. I wouldn't call it operating. He signs the
expense vouchers and whimpers about the costs. You know
Meul. He's an accountant—suspicious of anything that

costs less than a million or more than a billion and complains about everything in between." Sofer looked back at Marvina and grinned. Looking down at her lap, he said, "I hope that won't go off accidentally."

"Oh, I'll put it away."

Carpenter snapped, "You do as I tell you!"

"He's right, you know." Sofer added, "Never lose your advantage. Especially now when you know someone somewhere intends to kill you."

She was silent, both hands clutching the pistol and pressed down against her lap so the shaking wouldn't be seen.

They were in Washington, the limousine slowing around the curves of the Mall, the interior bathed in the yellowish glow from the lights of the monuments. The smoggy mucilaginous atmosphere hung in dirty drops.

"Who do you have at the Agency?" Carpenter asked.

"A secretary. A limited source. All she has is official information that is permitted for leaks."

"They know she's a leak?"

"I think so. It's either that or they operate like we do and assume everyone leaks and the only information available is what they want available or feel is safe or not harmful."

"Or to their advantage."

"Right." Sofer smiled.

"Hasn't changed, has it?"

"You didn't expect it to, did you?"

Carpenter shook his head. The driving, the concentration on the twists of the city's roads, the stop-and-go traffic made his body ache. He was bored with Sofer; there was no new information. There had been only one surprise. Even at this, he had already considered that Marvina had become the focus of Operation Little Girl. But he had dismissed it. Why Marvina? he wondered. It would be in the missing file. He'd have to think about it. He parked the limousine, still several blocks from his house. "We're going to get out here," he said.

"Here?" Sofer asked.

Carpenter paused before answering, troubled by the tone of Sofer's surprise. It had an element of disappointment. The question seemed wrong. A better question to fit the tone would have been, *Why not there?* And that raised the problem of where *there* was. "Why not?" Carpenter finally responded. He decided that Sofer had done nothing but lie. Everything learned from him had to be discarded.

"I thought you were going to your house."

"I am. Later."

"What about *me*?" Marvina asked, panic in her voice.

Carpenter half turned. "You'll be better off with me." He opened his door. "Alex, I want you to take it from here. I stripped it of its radio and communications system. I'd like it to stay that way. Leave it in front of the house. Pick a new driver and have him in the car at eight o'clock in the morning. I want the driver to wait exactly five minutes with the motor running. If I need transportation, I'll use it then. Otherwise, have him take it to the office and wait." Standing, he held the door, waiting for Marvina to join him outside. He watched Sofer slide across the seat and place himself behind the wheel. Satisfied that the move was not too hurried and was not threatening, he slammed the door.

"Take care of yourself," Sofer said.

Carpenter barely heard the parting words. He and Marvina had already reached the shadows of the building across the street. He held her motionless as he watched Sofer look up and search for them, the bald head swinging like a lantern.

The limousine finally pulled away, slowly moving up the street.

He took the pistol from Marvina, placed it on safety, and crammed it in his belt.

"You don't trust anyone at all, do you?"

"No," he said. He wondered if he would ever tell her about her father who had trusted and was now dead. He took her by an elbow and led her up the street at a rapid pace.

"Where are we going?"

"Don't talk. You'll need your energy."

"Jesus," she said softly, sounding more supplicating than frustrated. She became increasingly breathless as they moved along the street in a trot.

He suddenly stopped, pulling her back against the deep night shadow of the massive building on their left. Up the block, a street away, parked in front of his house, was the limousine. The motor was still running, the headlights burning. "Stay here," he said. He edged forward, along the building, each step noiseless.

He turned the corner and ran across the street, then up the block parallel to his own. He stopped and stood a moment, staring at his street. The limousine's headlights were out; the motor off. Sofer was standing on the sidewalk studying Carpenter's house; the streetlight shone off the top of his head.

Carpenter quickly ducked into a doorway when Sofer started walking toward him with a slow jauntiness, the picture of a casual pedestrian. "Psst," he exhaled sharply when Sofer was opposite him across the street. There was no sign that he had heard. Waiting until Sofer had gone to the corner and crossed the street, making the turn, he removed the pistol from his belt, unlatched the safety, and then followed. With a few quick steps he caught up.

Sofer looked at the pistol that Carpenter had in his right hand.

"Insurance?" he asked.

"I'll need it later." Carpenter stuck it back in his belt. "What did you see?"

"The curtain downstairs was pulled aside."

"That's sloppy."

"They don't know you. They'll get better as they learn. Where did you leave the girl?"

Carpenter was surprised at the question. "She's safe." He decided there was no reason to feel surprise, for that implied that he trusted Sofer. He knew what the question really meant. Sofer had secreted a transmitter on himself: the conversation was being heard.

"I didn't tell you everything about Little Girl before."

"Tell me now," Carpenter said very softly.

"Your mail drop with the prostitute was known, but covering it was fucked up. They got a copy of that letter, but they didn't stop it. Fuller's daughter was supposed to be picked up last night. You know how it is. Lessy didn't like family. When someone tripped, everybody went, the whole family."

"She doesn't know about Fuller."

Sofer shrugged. "Doesn't make a difference."

"Where are the orders coming from?"

"The White House."

"I can't put it together. The little bastard is too dumb for this. But then I never was good at putting things together. I just do the things that have to be done and I don't think about them. Who's your contact there?"

"Basset."

"If Lessy is part of this in any way, try to get a message to him. Tell him, I figure we're even. He killed Fuller, but I ruined him. That's good enough. Tell him to leave the girl alone."

"It's no good, Wes. I already know that. There's no deal. I was told that it's too late. They want you, both of you."

"Thanks . . . for the information."

"Don't thank me." Sofer looked away. "They wanted you to have it."

The conversation was over. Sofer kept going at the same slow pace. When he reached the corner, he glanced up quickly at the street sign, then crossed.

Carpenter watched him as he disappeared into the gloom. He wondered what Sofer had been promised for his allegiance; it might be no more than the desire to be on the winning team. That was reasonable.

There wasn't much time. He turned sharply and jogged down the street, stopping when he could see his house. Studying the windows as Sofer had done earlier, he continued on with a casual gait. The dark windows told him what he had expected. The curtain had indeed been pulled aside in one downstairs window. It was a pity about Sofer; he was bright and good on details, important characteristics. But he never questioned orders. He was only as good as the person who gave the orders. Who would have sent people into the house and then withdrawn them after leaving a symbol of their presence for Sofer to report? It took an enormous ego to be so certain that the trick would work. Carpenter walked on.

Marvina was still waiting in the shadowy recess where he had left her. "Where on earth—?"

"Not yet," he interrupted. "We'll be safe in a few minutes."

"For the night?"

"Not that long."

CHAPTER SEVEN

"If you don't think it's safe, why are we going?" she asked.

"It's safer than anywhere else," he said. He closed the back fence gate after she entered and leaned against it, staring at the house. They were two shadowy figures standing quietly at the rear of the dark town house, speaking in whispers, their attention on the building.

"If we're going to talk," he said, "we have to do it now. The chances are the house is completely wired."

"Wired?"

"Listening devices. The bedroom and the living room always were wired, tripped on by human voices, then recorded."

"Why didn't you remove them?"

"Better to let them stay. They only got what I wanted them to have."

"Who's they?"

"Everybody. Everybody does it to everybody."

"You do it, too?"

"It never made sense to me. When everybody does it, nobody says anything except what they want you to know."

She turned toward him for a moment, then back to the house.

"Are you hungry?" he asked. "There's food inside, but we have to be quiet."

"I don't know if my rumbling stomach can be quiet enough."

"You'll be surprised at how silent you can be when your life is at stake."

She didn't say anything, staring up into the black sky.

"Are you all right?" he asked.

"No," she answered, her whisper throaty. "I don't understand."

He reached a hand to her face and touched her damp cheeks. "We'll make it. Minute by minute we'll make it and then it will be behind us. That's the way it always is. Never knew it to fail."

He didn't know whether he was being truthful. The words sounded to him as though they should be comforting. He had never felt the need to say anything like them before.

"I'll be all right," she said.

"Sure?"

Her head bobbed up and down. "I'd like to know why, that's all. The whole world—my world—has suddenly become crazy. I don't know whether to be angry or scared. I've ended up being just scared. And that makes me angry."

"Stay angry," he said, "and stay scared. Both are good. Together they are a kind of pride." He touched her arm and they moved toward the house.

He led the way through the darkness, trailing a hand behind him that she held.

The interior was not entirely black, but had a hazy dim quality, some exterior light filtering from windows. There was an openness on the ground floor, rooms easing into rooms without thresholds or doors, the furniture along the walls looming in shapeless and colorless dark hulks. The silence was so complete that the rooms seemed empty. It made the darkness airless.

As he led her along, he became conscious of her breathing, aware that the shallowness of her breaths signaled fear. He paused and waited until her respiration was somewhat normal. She seemed to understand the reason for the pause and made no objection. He felt pleased with her. Excluding her first objections during the business of the driver, she had done what she was told. She seemed to understand that survival was dependent upon him. There would be a time when she would panic, he felt. He squeezed her hand. She squeezed back.

She could be his daughter, he thought, not Fuller's. If his life had been different, if only his life had been vastly different, if the world had not changed to what it now was. But these were thoughts better kept for other places. It was too late, he told himself. He felt the warmth of her hand, very small in his, and stopped wondering why he had accepted her father's request to care for her. Owen Fuller's friendship had been a weak motive, a convenient reason to center his hatred on Lessy, who had given him this life.

Leading her to the kitchen, he left her and softly ran his hands over the surfaces of the cabinets and the appliances. He shook his head sadly when he was done. The house had not only been wired, it had been boobytrapped. Nothing could be opened in the kitchen without detonating the invisible charges. He had felt the small ridges of plastic material inlaid in each hinge. That meant that even the toilet seats could be deadly surprises. He was angry with himself for not having anticipated this. It was not a logical nor typical Lessy maneuver. This was completely tight, with little chance of error. There was no leeway now. No assumptions could be made that the mind behind it would tolerate cracks through which they might escape.

Someone was afraid, he decided. He went to Marvina and took her hand again. In the beginning, he felt her resistance when he tried to lead her from the kitchen. Yet her reluctance to follow eased as he pressed her hand more firmly.

It was going to be a bad night, he decided. A tight operation meant the area outside was closed off. He and Marvina were within the ring of coverage. Somewhere outside the designated area they had left the limousine and had gone on foot. If he were alone, it would be no problem. But it wasn't just Lessy behind it, if Lessy was still alive and in the country. It was too big. Lessy would prefer fewer people, a more intensive operation, one in which his wits were totally involved and he could prove his personal superiority. He wanted it to be Lessy. It could be Lessy.

They went out even more quietly than they had entered. Marvina gave his hand a squeeze before she let go.

"What was wrong?" she whispered.

"The house is boobytrapped."

"Jesus. They want to kill us that badly?" He could feel her sink with fear.

"Looks like it. That's going to make it that much tougher to find a place tonight. Someone's going to a lot of trouble."

He closed the fence gate and began walking quickly down the alley to the street. She had difficulty keeping up with him and he slowed to permit her to catch up.

"I don't know if we can do it together," he said.

"What are we supposed to be doing?"

"Breaking out of this. You must have noticed, there hasn't been a car since we came. Nothing's moving. That means a cordon."

"Oh, my God!" She stopped.

He turned and studied her. "Once we get out we'll have the whole city. They won't be able to stop us."

"I'm glad you said *we*."

That settled that, he thought. He felt a twinge of shame for having considered separating for even a short while. She could never make it alone, no matter how detailed his directions. *"You must learn to take care of yourself,"* his father had told him. *"No one else gives a damn. No one. I don't. I don't give a shit about you."*

She didn't know anything like that, he remembered.

The street appeared empty, except for the wooden barrier and the flickering lantern beneath. They had spent fifteen minutes dodging from shadow to shadow to make five blocks' progress. Carpenter judged that the area of movement was limited to perhaps ten blocks long, three wide. He carefully searched the dimness ahead—the house alcoves, the parked cars, the black glassy windows of the homes, the flat roof of the end building across the way.

"Can you see anybody?" she asked.

"No," he answered, "but I know where he is."

"Who is?"

"The sniper. It's not going to be easy. Even if I manage to draw him out and we cross the street, the rest of them will shift and close the next block off. Then we won't have a chance. We would have better odds if we separated, if you were to go back and escape when they go past you to tighten the cordon around me. Stick to the shadows and duck when you hear a car or footsteps. I can move fast enough to be beyond them. They'll never know how you got out."

"No," she said.

He paused. The images of the escape collapsed in his head. "You'll never make it otherwise."

"I'll go with you."

"We'll be dead if you don't listen."

"I will." She removed her shoes. "When do we start?"

He patted her back. "When I say to, go like hell, head across the street and keep going. But first I'm going to boost our odds. Remember, no matter what happens, keep going."

"I'll remember."

They eased forward along a brick path, at the front of a home, hidden in the deep shadows. Carpenter estimated the chances of extinguishing the streetlights at the corner. There were two illuminating the place they were to cross. Any activity would begin the tightening of the noose.

He screwed on the silencer and held the .38 steady against the edge of the building. The silencer would cost him a small degree of accuracy—too much, he decided. He couldn't afford to miss and removed it, then aimed again.

Two quick explosions and the lights were out.

"Go!" he said.

As Marvina set out directly, he walked forward. He saw the movement on the roof and calmly raising the revolver, he sent a slug in its direction. Picking up the lantern under the roadblock, he looped it high toward the roof and fired again. There was a splatter of bullets behind him.

With the sound of a dull plop the lantern came down on the rooftop and flames broke out. For a second Carpenter saw the dark figure outlined. There was just enough time: he killed him, cradling the gun with both hands as he squeezed off the shot.

Marvina was waiting. They turned right at the first corner, then left at the one after. He knew what the next step was; the pursuers would try to box them up again. He could hear engines roaring to life somewhere behind them. He pulled the silencer from his pocket and reattached it as they ran. One of the vehicles was up ahead. He heard it screech to a stop. A door slammed, then the car sped off again.

Grabbing Marvina's arm, he brought her to a stop and pushed her flat against a well-lighted residential building. There was no darkness for hiding. Quiet and motionlessness were the only defenses.

A fat man turned the corner. He studied their street. The direction of his stare seemed to indicate that he saw them.

They didn't move. He took two fast steps toward them, gun raised. The man seemed to know that he had taken too long. He raised his other hand in a gesture of futility as he fell back, clutching instinctively at the path the unheard bullet had taken through his chest.

"Doesn't it bother you?" she asked, late that night as they sat on the steps of the Lincoln Memorial.

"Doesn't what bother me?"

"You've killed three people in the last fifteen hours."

"Five," he corrected, "if you count the day before. There were two near your office."

"My God," she muttered to herself.

Lessy had said it, he remembered, and not his father as he had thought for years. Although it was the sort of thing his father could have said: *"Some win and some lose. If you lose, you better be dead. I don't want to see you. I don't care a shit if you lose."* It was supposed to have been a comforting talk delivered after Carpenter had killed his first man, years ago.

There were a dozen other couples scattered up along the stairs. There had been more but the decreasing temperature was slowly driving them away.

"Doesn't it bother you?" she repeated.

"Yes," he answered.

Their eyes met. "You know more than you're telling me," she said.

Wondering at what he had said aloud and what he had said within himself, he knew that he wasn't able to judge what she knew. In a short time, he realized, he wouldn't be able to discern whether thoughts now in his mind had been said. It was disturbing. It had been better when he was totally alone. "I don't think so," he said, uncertain of what he meant.

"I don't know anything," she said.

He was content to leave it at that, for he didn't know whether it was true or not.

A few couples were strolling the mall between the Memorial and the Washington Monument, little dim figures reflected in the vast pool separating the two. Even as it grew cooler, the air seemed misty, the lights seemed to be halations, their distinction as individual electric beings smeared away.

He blinked several times and the air appeared to clear.

"What are we going to do?"

The question was a puzzle. They were going to stay where they were.

"We can't stay here," she added.

"Tonight we will," he said.

She contemplated his words without argument. "I suppose it's safer."

He nodded.

"What about tomorrow?"

"Someone wants to keep us away from the Senate hearing. We're going to be there."

"Why?"

"Because someone doesn't want us to." He looked at her face. It wasn't much of an answer, but there wasn't any other. She showed her dissatisfaction, her lips in a pout, her eyes flickering thoughtfully.

The steps emptied as people drifted away, and the mall below was vacant. Carpenter nudged Marvina and they moved up to the top of the Memorial and sat on one of the benches. She leaned next to him and closed her eyes. Her body shivered. He put an arm around her, protecting her from the night's chill.

It was three in the morning.

CHAPTER EIGHT

He wasn't asleep; he knew that. He could see as well as feel his daughter tucked against him for warmth, and he was aware of the early morning light filtering into the chamber, making the marble Lincoln look icy and stern. There was someone sitting on the bench in the far corner . . . or there seemed to be.

"What the hell are you doing with her?" the darkness said.

He looked down at the head of soft hair resting against his chest. "She's mine," he said. "She's my daughter. I'm taking care of her."

Marvina stirred a moment and then returned to quiet sleep.

"Don't bullshit me, boy. Nothing belongs to you. Not a Goddamned thing in this world. I'm giving you a loan of your life and I want it back with interest."

"Don't worry. I'll pay you back."

"In the meantime, I'll hold her for collateral." The darkness rose and came toward him. "I'll take her," it said as it came closer.

Carpenter held tightly to her, unwilling to let her go. As the figure approached, he suddenly knew who it was. It wasn't his father. The heavy, thick-lidded darkness had become Lessy.

He removed his arm from around Marvina and stood up, alert for battle.

He was uncertain whether he was awake or asleep. Marvina was standing next to him. She was clutching at his arm as he prepared to meet Lessy. "It's all right," he said, looking at her frightened face. When he turned to confront Lessy, Lessy was gone. The Memorial was empty, save for the two of them. He had been dreaming.

"Is it time to go?" she asked.

"Time to go," he said.

After eating breakfast at a luncheonette, Carpenter shaved in its bathroom with newly purchased gear, tossed it away when he was finished, collected Marvina, paid the check, and hailed a taxi out front.

"We're still early," Marvina said. "We could walk to the Capitol."

"We're not going yet."

She looked concerned, but climbed into the vehicle without further comment.

The cabbie, a frizzy-haired old black man, had an accepting nature. He didn't flinch when told to circle the Capitol "and be ready to duck if someone shoots at us." He had the look of a man who had seen it all and was neither worried nor interested.

Carpenter recognized one of the faces of the men standing at the top of the Capitol steps. He had seen him only once, coming out of Lessy's office. Flat faced, with black greasy hair, the man showed stunning white teeth in an ever-present smile. He had the occupational habit common to professional assassins: shifting eyes in a rigid unmoving head.

There was a large stream of people entering the building, workers and visitors. The other entrances were probably also covered, Carpenter decided.

"You saw somebody you knew," she said.

He was not as surprised that she was aware of his facial changes and able to decipher them, as he was disturbed by his revealing information. He wondered what had given him away. "I saw one," he said. "That probably means more."

"They wouldn't dare do anything here," she said.

"There are ways."

"Does that mean we can't go in?"

"It means that we'll have a problem." He was confused momentarily when she suddenly smiled. "*I'll* solve it." The smile was gone. "We'll solve it," he conceded. The smile returned. The magic word was *we*. That was disconcerting; he had always made his decisions alone.

"Maybe we shouldn't go in," she said.

"Maybe we shouldn't."

"If we went inside, we'd be safe, wouldn't we?"

"It's never safe, anywhere. You might say we would be relatively safe." He hated this discussion. He would never have had it if he were by himself. He would go inside because he was expected; there was no other choice. It wasn't safety that normally concerned him. Now it did.

He told the cabbie to make a turn away from the Capitol, then another turn and then another and another. His gray eyes narrowed as they passed a parked ambulance. Its driver was sitting idle, smoking a cigar, holding a microphone. There was a livid purplish scar on his forehead.

At the next light, two streets past the ambulance, he paid the cab driver and pushed a reluctant Marvina into the morning crowd. "Walk slow and keep going," he said, and turned back in the direction of the ambulance, ducking his head, slumping his frame to reduce his height. It was no good. Marvina was soon walking beside him. She looked determined. He decided not to argue.

"The ambulance," she said.

"We are going to use it, yes. What makes you so bright?"

"I was watching your eyes when you spotted it."

"I'm glad that's all it was."

"The man with the scar—"

"You were watching more than my eyes."

"Do you know him?"

"He's called the Doctor. He does odd jobs. Lessy once assigned him to take care of a man I kidnapped in Argentina. An American businessman. Lessy had the Doctor kill him to stir up trouble."

"That bothered you?"

"Lessy lied to me. That bothered me."

It was all right to kill, he told himself. That's the way it was now, like it or not, bothered or not bothered. What difference did it make anymore? Only Fuller had expressed doubts. He glanced at Marvina; she was studying his eyes. He felt guilty and dropped his gaze to the sidewalk in front of them.

"We're almost there," she said.

"There'll be someone in the back of it. I'll take care of the Doctor first. Attract his attention on this side and draw him over. I don't give a damn how. There's a good chance he'll recognize you, though. He's quick."

She nodded, and he quickened his step, and moved ahead of her. He slipped around the end of the ambulance at a run, circling it, and heard her banging on the side and shouting for help. The timing was off. The Doctor had seen him coming in the side mirror and wasn't paying attention to her.

Too late. Too late to stop.

He pulled at the door on the driver's side. The Doctor was grinning at him. The impact of a bullet struck the door and swung it out wide. Marvina was suddenly screaming. She had the door open on the other side.

He had the moment he needed as the Doctor turned to

push away Marvina's grasping hands. He broke the Doctor's nose with his first blow and then sliced the Adam's apple with the heel of his hand. He took the gun and pulled the apoplectic Doctor out by the scruff of his jacket and toward the rear of the ambulance. Holding him as a shield, he opened the door.

The attendant cowering back in the corner fired twice, each time hitting the Doctor. Carpenter himself was very careful not to miss. The interior of the ambulance was splattered red when he slid the Doctor inside and closed the door.

An ashen-faced young man, clutching a brief case, stood unmoving on the sidewalk staring at Carpenter. If others had noticed the activity, there was no sign of interest.

"Keep moving, please," Carpenter told the young man, making it sound like his civic duty. Eyes wide, the youth fled.

"That was perfect," he told Marvina when he returned to the cab of the ambulance and slipped behind the wheel.

"I didn't know what else to do," she said, looking pale but excited.

The radio speaker, crackling with static, asked what was going on, demanding a report.

He stared at the transceiver, wondering if it was useful to him. Would a confusing report be any more helpful than no report? He retrieved the mike that had fallen to the floor and pushed the "on" button. "Carpenter and the girl are dead. Have medical help ready. I'm wounded and going in."

The radio voice screeched: "What happened? For Christ's sake, what happened?"

Carpenter pulled the wires out and the screech abruptly stopped. He turned the key in the ignition, started up, and pulled into the traffic.

"Will that change anything?" she asked.

"I doubt it. It's standard to keep an operation under way until the group leader gives an all-clear signal. And he'll hold off until he sees the bodies. There might be enough doubt in his mind to give us a few minutes we need."

"I think we've done well so far, even if I don't understand why we did it."

"It was a standard, not very original operation for a public kidnapping. As we enter the building, we're hit with darts containing a tranquilizer, or something worse. When we fall, the man at the entrance rushes over, makes certain there aren't any good samaritans to interfere while he signals the ambulance with a lapel mike. The Doctor arrives, moves us into the back of the ambulance, and finishes us off."

"My God! You like this," she said. "You're really enjoying this."

"You're looking at my eyes again."

She looked away.

He wondered if she was right. He didn't think that she was. He remembered his father in a rage searching the house for him to punish him for breaking a plate: *"You little son of a bitch, I'll break your fucking hands when I catch you."* When finally trapped, he had attacked first and hit his father with a broom handle. He had been twelve years old and had beaten his father unconscious. He hadn't enjoyed that, but he recognized the sense of excitement, the flushing warmth, the fast heartbeat, the tension. It was still the same.

He left the heavy traffic at the first opportunity and drove northwest, finally found a small men's shop, and double-parked in front. Marvina followed him into the shop.

They bought two oversized black heavy loose slickers and black rubber rain hats and a pair of high rubber boots

for Marvina. Putting them on without comment, they left
the questioning salesman, who followed them out of the
store to look at the sky.

They drove away. He wondered if she understood. Her
face was smug and content. She had become more than a
daughter he had been protecting; she had changed. Fuller
would have been astonished by the transformation of their
daughter. He was doing it again; he was inserting himself
into a relationship that was nonexistent.

"Why are you smiling?" she asked.

"Was I smiling? You know, you make me uneasy sometimes the way you keep watching me."

"You *were* smiling. It wasn't the one you usually have,
like after you beat them. It was really a very pleasant
smile."

His smile vanished as he remembered. The training was
over and Lessy dragged a chair to the middle of the small
circle. He put his fat leg on it, the pants cuff rising to show
a narrow scar above the sock. "Listen, you fucks, there's
one thing I want to say. You're working for the company
now. There's *them* and there's *us*. It's that fucking simple.
And I'm the guy who tells you who *them* is. That's Lessy's
Law. Remember it."

It was Fuller who said afterwards, "He thinks like you
do, Carpenter. He's a paranoid, too."

He left the ambulance at a taxi stand in the front of the
Capitol and they got out. The agent he knew was standing
at the top of the steps. Taking Marvina's elbow, he maneuvered her among an ascending group of tourists. He felt
and heard the wack of a dart striking his poncho just as he
stepped among the others. The sniper must have fired out
of frustration, realizing that the designated targets were
slipping out of his control. There was now a new element
Carpenter had to consider: desperation. It would bring
both advantage and danger. The original plan to stop him

and Marvina would be abandoned, supplanted by reflexive action.

Greasy Hair was descending, coming at him. The tension of the moment was evident on his face; its muscles had tightened into a rictus of determination. There could be no mistakes now.

He released Marvina's elbow and swung his arm back, stepping to the side, knowing that he was momentarily a target again. He went directly at Greasy Hair, confronted him for a split second, and then sidestepped. A dart flattened on the stair below and bounced away, making a short cracking sound. Greasy Hair looked down.

Carpenter smashed the man in the groin. There was a look of quick surprise on the face and then the eyes closed as the pain of the blow began to double him up. Carpenter twisted around and grabbed the falling man by his collar and held him facing down the stairs. The only sound was the shuffling of shoe leather and a quiet breathless groan. A dart hit the helpless man and he finally managed to say, "You bastard," but it was little more than a whisper.

He let him drop.

A Capitol policeman, approaching rapidly, reached out for the slumping assassin and missed.

"I couldn't hold him," Carpenter explained. "He must have had a heart attack." He didn't wait for a reaction. He climbed the last steps and joined Marvina.

Once inside the massive entrance hall, Marvina hooked an arm in his. "What did you do to him?"

"Not much. He was hit by a dart."

"He was rolling all the way down."

"I think that'll upset him."

As they walked they removed their rain gear. Marvina found another dart embedded in the loose arm flap and showed it to Carpenter.

"We were lucky," he commented, and she nodded. They

stuffed the rubber clothing under a bench and went seeking a hall that would take them from the visitor's area.

They were still early when they reached the committee room. There were the standard people milling about in the rear; the mandatory gaggle of visitors, newsmen, congressional aides, wives. The representatives of the television media were already in place. A cameraman shot some footage of Carpenter and Marvina Peters as they wove down the center aisle to the front table. Several senatorial assistants, standing in conversation, looked up quickly when they saw the two, and the level of hubbub increased.

When neither of the two assistants left the room, Carpenter felt momentary relief. They obviously didn't know that someone had tried to prevent his appearance.

"Are we safe now?" Marvina asked, very casually.

"Probably. It's impossible to be certain."

"You don't seem to be worried."

"I'm always worried."

"Did we have a choice? Of being here, I mean."

"I assumed we didn't."

There was a burst of laughter among the reporters. Carpenter's head snapped in its direction. Laughing wasn't threatening, he told himself. He had to relax. There would be tension enough later.

CHAPTER NINE

Roose was the first to appear. Before sitting down, he arranged a pile of papers and looked over at Carpenter. He wasn't smiling; he seemed to want to establish Carpenter's location and nothing else. No surprise, no anticipation, Carpenter noted. After he had completed his task with the papers, he sat and stared, motionless and sightless, the hooded eyebrows revealing nothing. He had the look of a man about to go through a senseless routine.

Slowly senators began arriving. One entered, helped by an aide. A ruddy-faced man, the senator's eyes were glazed and his legs unsteady. Once settled, he promptly closed his eyes and fell asleep. The committee chairman bustled into the room once, glanced at the empty seats, and left again. Within four minutes all the front committee chairs were filled save one. Absent was the senator from Idaho.

The chairman turned and glared at the empty chair and seemed reluctant to begin. He gaveled the room to order.

"The meeting will come to order. The committee counsel will proceed."

"Mr. Carpenter," Roose began, "there's been a rumor since your appearance yesterday that you wouldn't be here today. Is there any reason you can offer why a rumor of that nature might have gotten started?"

"It never crossed my mind," Carpenter said. "I was determined to be here regardless of difficulty."

"Did you have any difficulty?"

Carpenter glanced at Marvina. "What sort?" he asked.

"Did anyone suggest that it might be better if you didn't make an appearance today?"

"No, sir." He was conscious of Marvina rustling her handbag, indicating displeasure with his answer.

The chairman nudged Roose and leaned over to the counsel to whisper something, his hand covering the mike in front of him. He sat back, then leaned forward. "I want it on the record, Mr. Carpenter, that I am pleased that my faith in the power and function of this great body is and remains intact, and that rumor to the contrary, no one would dare suborn its intentions."

Carpenter touched Marvina to calm her. The worst that could be done at that moment was to raise questions in Congress about its stable control of any situation. Its members didn't want to know about any situation that might bring a confrontation with the freewheeling violence of the country's espionage apparatus. Congress would hunt for material that it could handle, no more. It would be upset and probably attempt to punish anyone who offered more.

Roose studied the chairman, apparently waiting to see if another interruption was forthcoming. Chairman Dobentz nodded that he was done, and the counsel turned to the witness. "That settles the rumor, then."

"Yes, sir," Carpenter said.

"I'd like to deal with your resignation from government service. We'd like to find out if there is a relationship between it and the Lessy-Fuller business, and the shocking destruction of the Farbie Building. I'm sure you understand that a serious accusation was made against you yesterday."

"I'd like to answer that accusation."

"You will have an opportunity, Mr. Carpenter, in the context of the questioning. But first, your resignation and its relationship with the other matters."

"I didn't realize that those matters were joined. I certainly didn't know that Roland Lessy's files had been moved to the Farbie Building." Carpenter hesitated. Something was wrong. Hawk-faced Roose seemed to be telling him to be quiet. A warning?

"All of these seem to be joined," Roose said. "The distinguished senator from Idaho and his staff made an analysis of Mr. Kulbers's testimony. There seems to be a clear connection." His voice had dropped as though he were talking personally to Carpenter. He was prompting.

The sleeping senator began suddenly to snore, and for a moment his wheezes and nasal explosions made his mike howl shrilly. An assistant moved the microphone and tapped the senator on the shoulder.

Carpenter whispered to Marvina, "What's up? Have you read the Kulbers testimony?"

"Up until yesterday's testimony, yes. As far as I know, Kulbers is just an office manager."

Carpenter tensed. He began to understand as he remembered the senator from Idaho making the impassioned accusation. Today was going to be a repeat of the first day. If Roose and the committee chairman had been on his side, they had lost a battle during the night. That also explained why the entire committee was attending. The battle was over and it was important to show publicly that they were on the winning side. Not my side, Carpenter thought.

Roose was studying him, seemingly hesitant to continue. The attorney wiped his face with a handkerchief. Carpenter wondered what had happened during the night.

Roose looked up. "Before I continue," he said, "I feel I should explain what was discovered. The Farbie Institute was in the midst of an analysis of Mr. Lessy's department. Apparently it was a routine internal check. All departments undergo similar investigations every few years."

So that was it, he thought. Kulbers had inadvertently let

slip the information that Lessy's material was housed in the Farbie Building. It was more than that, he sensed, but it wasn't critical yet. He groped for the direction being taken. There had to be misdirections he could give to sidetrack the inquiry. When none came, he had an impulse for violent action, as though it might help. His body was rushing with blood and his muscle tissue twitched involuntarily. Time, time. Give me time, he heard his inner voice say.

Roose was saying, "If someone wanted a look at Roland Lessy's material, the Farbie Building was obviously the place to go."

"May I ask a question?"

Carpenter looked at Marvina when she made this sudden interruption. It was as if she had heard his plea.

"Yes, of course, Miss Peters." Roose was also surprised.

Her face was taut, drained. She seemed to sense Carpenter's need for delay, her eyes skittering from him to Roose, back and forth, focusing on neither. "If it becomes necessary to advise my client, and as you may have noticed, he doesn't require much . . ."

There was a burble of laughter in the room, little pockets of appreciative murmurs.

Her face reddened.

"Go on, Miss Peters."

"I would like on the record a concise statement of the committee's purpose in this hearing. It strikes me that sometimes direction becomes lost if this isn't done."

Carpenter was grateful for the time, but it didn't help. He couldn't decipher the meeting, he couldn't put it together.

The committee chairman, Senator Dobentz, sat up to his mike. He stared at Marvina Peters contemptuously.

The room was quiet.

"Do you understand what you have just said, young lady?"

The whirr of the electric clock on the wall was the dominant sound. Even the sleeping senator opened his eyes and was wide awake. He appeared frightened.

"Yes, sir," she said.

Carpenter held his breath. She had given him some time, but he still couldn't put it together. He leaned to Marvina. "Thanks. It's no good. We'll just have to wait and see what happens. Just apologize."

Her eyes met his briefly and then she raised her head. "I'm very sorry, senator. I don't know where my manners went. I didn't mean to suggest that this committee was following an improper procedure or that its hearing could in any sense be improved. Please accept my apology."

Very good, Carpenter thought.

Dobentz seemed pleased. The hardness of his cheeks softened and became flab again. "I think, without fear of contradiction from the other members present, that the chair will do that very thing."

There was a restless murmur in the room followed by gaveling. The interruption was over, the testimony about to resume. Carpenter still couldn't guess where the questions would lead. His only instinct was to attack any reason he might have had to destroy the Farbie Building. He sensed that he had already lost.

Roose dabbed his face again. His eyes met Carpenter's. He seemed reluctant to continue. Finally he said, "If someone wanted a look at Lessy's material, I was saying, he would go to the Farbie Building."

Carpenter shook his head in disagreement.

"No matter what was learned from Mr. Kulbers, I don't believe Mr. Lessy's material ever left his office. He wouldn't allow it. I know Mr. Lessy. It would never have happened."

Roose stopped mopping with his handkerchief. He studied Carpenter and then turned to the chairman. The two whispered heatedly. Finally Dobentz nodded reluctantly. Roose stood and walked all the way around the enormous polished table and went to Carpenter. He moved the microphone away.

"Carpenter, listen to me. The game is almost over. I'm pleading with you. Open up on everything. Tell everything you know. Tell it all. Admit to everything. And let loose on Lessy. If you do, we can still save it. I'm convinced of it. The chairman will put his head on the block and introduce the letter he got from Owen Fuller. Members of the Congress are still wavering. If we can open it up for the American public with the press, we can swing it. I'm convinced of it. Lessy needs secrecy to pull it off. If we don't stop him today, Lessy will have it all by tomorrow. It's moving that fast." The attorney's eyes were calmly searching Carpenter's face, like a doctor at the bedside of a terminal patient.

Roose's words didn't help. They were describing nothing he understood. Carpenter only knew that he had himself, and now Marvina, to look after. It had always been himself. No one else cared.

"Don't you care what happens to this country?" Roose asked, his voice husky. "We're about to lose it to the secret agencies that were set up to protect us. In the darkness they got control of everything, and nobody out there knows yet. You can tell them who Roland Lessy is. They don't know. They don't know."

Carpenter shook his head.

"You know what the operational title is? You know what it means?"

"No."

"Operation Little Girl."

Carpenter studied Roose. He glanced at Marvina, who was looking worried. "It's all right. We'll do it *our* way."

Roose looked back at the chairman and shook his head. He said to Carpenter, "I'm sorry. It's going to get rough. There's nothing now." He left to return to his place.

"Were you aware of the makeup of the Farbie Institute?" Roose asked as he resettled himself.

"Makeup?"

"Personnel."

"Vaguely. I was aware that many of its people were retired CIA members."

"Were you aware that Lessy's predecessor at Clandestine Operations was in charge of investigations?"

"No, sir."

"Wouldn't that have made Lessy more amenable to the oversight of his material if he knew that it was in friendly hands?"

"I can't speak for him."

"Does it sound logical to you?"

"It sounds logical but . . ."

"But what?"

"Lessy wasn't a totally logical man. He was strong willed."

"Isn't it possible to be strong willed and also logical?"

"I suppose so. My experience with him indicated that logic was served until he decided that it ran counter to his personal ambition."

"Do you have examples?"

Carpenter studied all of the faces before him, finally settling on one, the senator from Florida. Lessy had done him a favor, removing one of his administrative assistants who was about to testify against him on corruption charges. That was logical, but that's not why Lessy had done it. The assistant had once put his hand on Lessy's knee during a friendly Congressional visit. *"That prancing little prick,"* Lessy had raged. *"He put his fucking hand on me. One excuse, just one, and he's dead."*

Carpenter looked back at the committee counsel. "The examples would affect national security," he said.

Roose closed his eyes, opened them, and shook his head in frustration.

"Is it our understanding that you were not informed that Lessy's papers were housed in the Farbie Building?"

"I was not in a position to be so informed. There's no reason I should have been told," Carpenter said.

"Did you know?"

"I assume that what you tell me is true."

"Did you know?"

"*No.*"

There wasn't any escape from it. ("Christ, can you imagine it, Wes?" Owen Fuller had said. "Kulbers dropped it at lunch. If Lessy knew, he'd kill Kulbers with his bare hands. Kulbers knows it, too. He's shitting in his pants. You know the administrative mind. He has a directive; he does it. Every damn thing Lessy ever put on paper is at the Farbie Building. Grab that and Lessy is done.")

A sandy-haired man had just entered the chamber behind the senators. He seemed to be excited that the room was filled with people, he was confused by the fullness. He spoke quietly to one of the aides at the side wall, then stared at Carpenter as if he had noticed him for the first time.

Carpenter attempted to sort out the face in comparison with other faces he had known and decided that it was new. Sandy Hair suddenly left.

He felt uneasy at the departure, wondering if it was meaningful. He was already disturbed that he had found it necessary to make an untruthful denial and decided that his concern about the man's coming and going might not be important.

Roose and Senator Dobentz had ducked their heads together in a private discussion.

"Why was that so important?" Marvina whispered.

"They're trying to tie me to blowing up the Farbie Building. I suppose they're convinced that I released the Lessy papers on Fuller."

"Whoever did it should be given a medal."

"It doesn't work that way. Hang on, there's something up."

Roose rose from his seat and went to the back door and spoke briefly to someone. He returned and nodded to the chairman. He looked determined. "Mr. Carpenter," he said, "I assume you can see the connection now."

"I saw the connection earlier. I hadn't until you brought the Kulbers evidence in."

"I'm glad it's clear."

"I didn't say it was clear. I said that I saw the connection. I'll go as far as saying that Lessy's disappearance, the Fuller business, and the destruction of the Farbie Building could be linked together."

"That's a beginning. Have you read this morning's paper, Mr. Carpenter?"

"No, sir."

"That's a pity."

Carpenter didn't respond to the comment. He understood the implication and wondered what it meant for him. Whatever it was, it had opened for the committee a line of questioning it hadn't had the previous day. From fishing in muddy water, the committee now seemed to have gone hunting, with a clear shot at the game. The chairman took over:

"Mr. Carpenter, the committee has another witness at this time. We want you to stand down until this new witness has finished. It will not take long. I'm sure you won't mind."

While he was taking a seat in the audience, he noticed

Alex Sofer ducking out of the hall. There were still a few minutes, he thought, before the surprise witness appeared and was sworn in. He told Marvina that he'd be right back and scurried after Sofer.

The hall was empty except for the guard and a line of visitors waiting to attend the hearing. He went to the men's room and turned on the cold water full blast while an elderly man was preparing to leave.

"What was in the paper?" he asked when the room was seemingly empty.

"You don't have a friend left." The voice came from one of the booths.

"I figured that last night."

"I'm sorry about that."

"I don't blame you. All I want to know: Is Lessy out there?"

"I don't know. The little bastard is. Isn't that bad enough? He has put Sy Basset on you. Don't let them shit you about Kulbers. Kulbers wouldn't tell the committee a fucking thing, even by inference."

"Kulbers doesn't bother me."

"The new witness will."

"That's no surprise."

He dipped his hands under the cold water and turned off the faucet. He dried his hands on a paper towel and left.

The new witness was a young woman. She was nervous, her eyes fixed on her hands as they clutched one another in white-knuckle tension. The oath was just being administered and she was concentrating on the words. When it was complete, she acknowledged it in a high-pitched voice.

Carpenter sat down next to Marvina and patted her knee. "Have I missed anything?"

"Not yet. I know what the papers said."

"Let me guess. It was a White House source saying that Kulbers had told me that Lessy's material was in the Farbie Building."

"Is it true?"

"Untrue."

"You're right except for the source. It apparently came out of the committee."

The new witness had difficulty paying attention and was showing some confusion in understanding Roose's first question. She apparently was expecting a different question and said, "No," when asked if she had worked for the Farbie Institute. She finally raised her eyes at the silence that met her answer. She didn't understand.

"Did I understand your answer?" Roose asked.

"I think so, sir." Her eyelashes fluttered.

"I don't think you did," he said. "Are you employed by the Farbie Institute?"

"Oh, I'm sorry. The answer is yes."

Relief. The senators smiled at one another.

"I thought you asked me if I was employed in the Investigative Branch."

"Are you?"

Smiling. "No."

"What do you do at the Institute?"

"I'm in the pool."

"Pool?"

"The secretarial pool."

"Were you working on the day the building was destroyed?"

"Yes."

"Did you see the individual who was responsible?"

"Oh. Yes, sir."

CHAPTER TEN

The senator from Idaho arrived just before the secretary completed her testimony. He and Sandy Hair stood watching as the girl turned and identified Carpenter. The senator was all bright shiny teeth in a brimming grin.

"Jesus," Marvina said when the secretary's manicured finger aimed at Carpenter. Heads turned to stare.

"Don't worry. She's a fake," he whispered.

"In the meantime . . ."

"Forget it. The committee's been had. As long as they think they have us here, we should be safe. That's good news, isn't it?"

"I hope so."

The woman from the Farbie Institute looked back as she left, confident of what she had done.

The senator from Idaho took his seat as Roose requested that Carpenter move forward again. Several members of the press ran out, presumably to catch deadlines with their new information.

Carpenter felt uneasy, not believing the comforting words he had just given Marvina. He wondered at his compulsion to assure her security, even when it served no purpose. He knew it was nonsense that he should feel protective toward her. She was not his daughter but, like everyone else, a stranger he happened to know, a potential danger. It didn't help. Fuller's daughter was also his. That was irritating, but it was true. At times he felt that she was his alone.

"Mr. Carpenter," Roose said, "I'm sure you found the testimony you've just heard somewhat interesting."

"Somewhat."

"Just somewhat?"

"I was using your word."

"How would you describe it?"

"Unlikely."

"Unlikely?" Surprise filled the attorney's face.

"I would think that an operation of the size of breaking into and blowing up the Farbie Building would require more than a lone man. Even if one man had been able to accomplish the feat, I'd seriously doubt that anyone would be able to recognize him."

"Since national security considerations limit precise examples, I wonder if you might give us some general ideas about your own professional experience with explosives. As we understand it, you're considered extremely adept with explosives. Isn't this true?"

"Extremely? That's flattering."

"You were adept at demolition."

"It was part of my training."

"It was a major duty for a time, I understand. Correct?"

"No, sir. It was never a major duty."

"You were involved in projects the size of the Farbie Building."

"Alone?"

"Alone."

"Never alone. It might be correct to say that I've participated in undertakings of the same magnitude."

The counsel was annoyed with the quibbling. "I'm only trying to show your capability in this area. I'm not accusing you."

"I heard someone accuse me. I'd like to make it clear that

there are reasons to suspect that such an accusation against me is ill founded. Earlier I pointed out that I didn't have any information that might have given me the motivation to obtain the Lessy documents to bring them to public attention. Perhaps this is as good a time as any to state that I have served a major part of my adult life in the Central Intelligence Agency and have never disputed its operations and philosophy as explained by Roland Lessy. The major suspicion against me—that I might now feel that the Agency has outlived its usefulness and should be destroyed—rests on my supposed friendship with Owen Fuller and my anger at his death. Mr. Fuller and I were roommates at Yale and we were both recruited by Mr. Lessy. I regarded him as something of an oddball, for he avoided field service when he could. This made for a very uncomfortable relationship since I had spent most of my time in the field."

The chamber was quiet. The senator from Idaho reached for his microphone.

"Mr. Carpenter, Mr. Carpenter. That's all very touching, but it doesn't answer anything. A young woman of sterling qualities has sat here before us and informed us that she saw you within the confines of the Farbie Building, in her words, 'throwing bombs into offices.' The press has done an admirable job in discovering that you were Owen Fuller's roommate at college and then in locating a cleaning woman who saw someone, answering your description, delivering forged copies of Lessy's memorandum to a newspaper office."

His speech given, he slumped back, but he never removed his eyes from Carpenter. It was apparent that he would continue, as necessary, to counter anything that Carpenter might say in defense of himself. He extended an arm and lolled it over the back of his chair. Waiting.

He must wait, too, Carpenter thought. The attack today

had been somewhat reasoned and certainly less hysterical. He wished he knew some background on the senator. As it was, he had only guesses based on what he had seen during the two sessions. One was troubling. Had the senator's absence in the morning meant that he didn't think Carpenter would attend? If true, did that mean the senator was party to the efforts to prevent Carpenter from attending?

Roose, too, was waiting. He stared at the chairman and didn't turn toward Carpenter until he received a nod.

"Let's go back to the beginning, Mr. Carpenter. I'm not clear as to the reasons you resigned from the CIA and when."

"I felt that it was unnecessary to retain membership after the role of the proprietary company I ran became known."

"MPI?"

"MPI."

"For the record, please tell us what those initials stand for."

"As you know, it was and is an export sales organization with worldwide offices. The initials stood for Motivational Production International."

"Its role as a cover organization became known two years ago. Is that right?"

"Yes."

"Did you resign then?"

"No."

"Perhaps you'd like to tell us why you didn't."

"Since it was a proprietary company, there were many arrangements that had to be terminated. It took time. It was advantageous to remain with the Agency during this period."

"When did you resign?"

"A month and a half ago."

"Allow me to put it in the context of events: Within a week of Owen Fuller's tragic death, prior to the demolition of the Farbie Building, the stealing and leaking of the Lessy documents about the Fuller death, you quit."

"I suppose that my resignation can be viewed among that set of events. The chronological order is correct."

"What was Roland Lessy's reaction?"

"He was upset."

"Mildly upset, somewhat upset, angrily upset?"

"I'm not sure I'm a judge."

"Really! You used the word 'upset.' Surely, if you knew that much, you should be able to categorize the degree of that upset."

"Roland Lessy was a man of strong passions and always seemed angry."

"Then how did you know he was upset?"

Carpenter shrugged. "He said he was."

"He said he was upset? Isn't that a rather mild word for a man who always seemed angry, a man of strong passions?"

"Yes, it is. My father . . ." He stopped, telling himself that he must be careful. Lessy. Lessy. Roland Lessy was the subject. He cleared his throat. "Roland Lessy was prone to use words that might shock most of those here. I think it's enough to say that he was upset."

The slip disturbed Roose.

Carpenter looked away, wondering why he had suddenly mentioned his father, remembering beating him, remembering the fury, the anger, followed by triumph. Lessy. Lessy is the subject. It was curious. The room was so quiet.

"Was your father also prone to language that might shock us?" Roose was obviously trying to sound understanding.

"He spent most of his adult life in a wheelchair. He found life very trying and used strong language."

Roose and Chairman Dobentz bent together and discussed something. They each continued to keep their sight on Carpenter. Then they separated. "We'll accept your word that Roland Lessy was upset. Perhaps you'll describe for us this moment of your resignation. We'll trust your continuing to be discreet concerning Mr. Lessy's language."

"Chairman, Chairman!" The senator from Idaho was slapping the table for attention. "I object!"

"Your objection, senator?" Dobentz asked.

"We're allowing this man"—he waved a stubby finger at Carpenter—"to picture a devoted servant of this government as a foul-mouthed unpleasant individual! I object! I have personally known Roland Lessy and have never found that he uttered any but the highest sentiments!"

(*"You fucking bastard! Nobody cuts and runs on me!"* Lessy had said, crumpling the resignation and dropping it to the floor. *"I got this damn government in the palm of my hand and you're not going to take it away. It's mine. I want you to remember that no one stops working for me unless I say so. And you don't make decisions, fuck face; I do!"* His sweating slab of a face, twisted with anger, had become an oily red. *"MPI is mine. I created it. I'm the one who picks where its money goes. I'm the one who fattens political campaigns. I'm the one who owns presidents! You don't do a fucking thing but follow my orders! You got that, jerk off? You remember that or I'll stick you back in the booby hatch and lose you. The Goddamned fucking sick minds! Yours is the worst!"*)

He closed his eyes for a moment. The tension wouldn't go. Lessy was staying with him, somewhere inside, continuing to torment his memory. The senator from Idaho was giving a speech about Lessy, his marvels and devotion to public service. It was foreign to Carpenter; his memory of Lessy was colored by the image of the heavy crude corpulence stomping out demands and orders and the bugged eyes that never seemed to blink or move.

When the senator finished his speech, the chairman

called for a short recess and left the room followed by Roose. Both looked troubled—tortured.

It was odd, he thought. Marvina made it possible to endure. That innocence, that had been so strange in the beginning, was now beguiling and needed protection even though it, the innocence, was partially gone. How gone? How much gone? He decided that he could never know, that she was whatever he believed her to be. His warmth for her, he realized, had become entwined with his need for her as a daughter, as someone who was part of him. Was it love to feel protective? He didn't know. He had never felt love; he had not felt this before.

"Your Mr. Sofer is here," she said.

He opened his eyes, staring first at her and finding that her eyes were directed behind him. He followed their direction and found Alex.

Sofer's lips were twirled around a finger as he bit on its nail. His bald head blushed when he noticed both Marvina and Carpenter studying him, and he removed the finger from his teeth. His body became rigid as he began to rise and then he sank back. He smiled.

Carpenter moved back to the rear of the hall and waited. Sofer rose and joined him.

"Who's listening?" Carpenter said.

"I'm clean. They wanted it that way."

"Who?"

"The little bastard and Sy Basset. They were afraid I might be picked up and I'd have to tell who was on the other end of the listening device. No one's worried that you'll escape. The outside is crawling. Inside, too. It won't be subtle this time. Everybody is upset about last night and this morning."

Carpenter smiled.

"Funny?"

"The word 'upset' is funny."

"I guess it is. The stupid bitches, they don't have any idea of what it was like to have Lessy talk to you."

"Where is he?"

"Who?"

"Lessy."

"I honestly don't know. I really did believe in the press speculation that he had gone over. It made sense. It's been impossible to tell one side from the other for years. Not like the old days. Then it mattered."

"I don't remember the old days."

"You're too young."

"They still want the girl?"

"No changes. As I told you, that was a Lessy idea originally. It started when you said you'd resign. He thought she mattered to you. I think he was hoping to turn you around, shatter your resolve. He never understood you. He thought you were like everybody else and could be reached if he found the right button to press."

He saw Marvina staring at them. She looked worried. Lessy was right, he thought. He was surprised that Lessy had turned out to be right, even if he had been wrong in the beginning. "I wonder," he began to say, and then became quiet. He wasn't certain that he could complete his sentence, for he didn't know what he wondered other than about Marvina. "Basset want you to stay here?"

"Those are my instructions. I'm supposed to call when the hearing ends today."

"I don't believe anything you tell me," he said.

"I don't blame you."

CHAPTER ELEVEN

The chairman and Roose returned, their look of torment still with them. Immediately upon reopening the hearing, Dobentz recognized the senator from Idaho.

The senator, aware that Carpenter was missing from the witness table, demanded that he return and listen. "I want Mr. Carpenter to hear every word I say. I want him there in that seat paying attention, so that he will know what my opinion of Roland Lessy is."

Carpenter returned to his place next to Marvina.

"What did you learn?"

"They're waiting for us outside in force and are going to fall on us hard."

"Hard?"

"No playing games."

"I didn't think they had been playing games," she said, her voice dry.

"Something more direct this time."

"Do you believe Sofer?"

"Only when it makes sense, when he tells me what I already feel and know. He said the little bastard's behind this and that he is taking orders from Sy Basset. I don't believe it."

The senator from Idaho pointed his finger at Carpenter again. He interrupted his own speech. "Mr. Chairman, I protest. He's not listening. He's not showing the necessary respect for these proceedings."

Dobentz tiredly stared at the senator, as if considering the importance of adding his own comments. He didn't, finally.

"Mr. Chairman, obviously Mr. Carpenter is not alone in his disrespect."

"Senator," the chairman said, "in my state there are many horses; they do not always drink when brought to water. The quality of the water has something to do with it."

There was applause and laughter. Dobentz gaveled ineffectually, allowing the outburst to decline at its own rate.

Before more comments were offered, the Senate vote bell rang. There was a look of relief among those at the head table.

The chairman briefly glanced down both ends of the table and then suspended the hearing until after lunch. The hearing was to be adjourned until two.

"Are we going to be safe here?" Marvina asked.

Carpenter looked behind him and saw Sofer hurry from the chamber before anyone else, in more haste than necessary. "Maybe not," he answered.

"Stick here. I want to find out where he's going. I won't be long." He brushed her concerned face with his finger tips. "Don't worry."

She forced a smile and touched him back.

He scurried up the aisle, pushing aside others who were leaving. He wasn't prepared. It was suddenly too late to react. There were arms on both sides of his body holding him, going with his movement, compressing him, a hand inside his suit coat, flapping on his chest, slipping down to his belt, finding and removing his gun. There was nothing to be done immediately in the crush of those exiting. The faces of the two were young and smooth, showing no emotion, just minor exertion. He wondered if Sofer had known what was planned. Probably not. They wouldn't have thought it necessary to tell him.

"Say a word and you die here," the one on his right said without changing his dull expression, hardly moving his lips.

The room's front exit doors weren't wide enough for the three of them. As one held back slightly, twisting Carpenter to force him through, a shriek to the rear of them froze everyone else.

"Carpenter! Stop them! God in Heaven, stop them!" It was Marvina.

The man on Carpenter's left twisted his head to see. Carpenter kicked his own legs back with all of his power. The men lost their grip and he fell between them, his arms free, and he grabbed the outside ankles on both sides and gave a massive pull. Both men tipped forward and dropped. The one on the left rose and began running. The man on the right landed on his shoulder and turned, a gun now in his hand. A Capitol guard brought his foot down hard on the man's wrist.

"Thanks," Carpenter said as he rose and retrieved the weapon. He stuffed the pistol in his belt. He was slightly out of breath.

"Hey, we'll need that for evidence."

"I need it more than you do." He saw Sofer at the end of the hall. There was dismay on his face.

Returning to the hearing room, he waved at Marvina, who was standing on her chair still screaming. She stopped when she saw him and began pushing through the shocked crowd toward him. She rushed into his arms.

"I'm okay. You saved my life."

"We did it," she said. She was crying, her head ducked against his breast.

He held her until she stopped.

Roose was standing, watching, and then he motioned for them to follow him.

There was a large office behind the hearing chamber. Roose cleared it of the curious aides and secretaries until just the three of them remained. Carpenter was still holding Marvina.

"You're lucky. The new group of Capitol police are in the process of taking over. We still have some of the old ones. This place will be buttoned up after lunch. It's already pretty tight."

"What happens now?"

"I don't know. The hearing goes on. That's all I know. I can tell you what's going to happen in a few days. The Vice President will resign. The betting is that Senator Wilby will be chosen as his successor by the President."

"Wilby, the senator from Idaho?"

"And Lessy will dominate everything without anyone being aware of what happened. We'll still have a President, a Vice President, a Congress, a Supreme Court, all the trappings of a civilized democracy, but it will belong to Lessy. Ever since Truman set up the CIA, this possibility has existed. All it needed was a Lessy."

"What are the chances of getting out of here alive?" Carpenter asked.

"Is that all that's on your mind?" Roose's eyebrows lifted. "For fuck sakes, Carpenter, you still don't understand. Lessy can't do it unless he has secrecy. At this moment you're the only one who can take that away from him. You can still do it this afternoon. Just tell the truth. I'll help. The chairman, Senator Dobentz, will help. Without you to tell the press the truth, it's lost. Senator Dobentz will fold. I can't do it; no one will believe me. I've already tried."

"We're going to make it out of here alive," Carpenter said, still holding Marvina. He released her and sat down.

He didn't understand what had been told him. He knew the words; Fuller had used them more than once and had seemed just as confused by his bewilderment. "If you're done," Carpenter said, "I'd appreciate it if you had some-one order us some lunch."

Roose, about to speak, kept his peace. Forlorn, he shook his head in frustration. "Sure," he said. "What the hell, you need your lunch. We'll just have to wait and see how it turns out. I'll send someone in," he said and left the room.

"I don't trust him," Marvina said.

"That makes two of us."

"Does any of what he said make sense to you?"

"I don't know," he said. "I haven't thought about it. Right now, the only thing I think about is for the two of us to stay alive. He's not helping us do that."

The first member of the committee who returned was the senator from Idaho. He was startled to see Carpenter and Marvina finishing lunch in the Senate office. "What the blazes are *you* doing in here?" he demanded.

Marvina stood up and swallowed.

"You have no business here!" he half shouted.

"Don't tell us that," she said. "Your friends tried to kill us out there." She pointed to the chamber door and then began to weep.

"Young woman, don't you make accusations at me. I know your games. Out! Out! You haven't been invited back here." He bustled forward, took her arm, and began to move her.

Carpenter reached out from his seat and grabbed the senator's wrist. "I'm not arguing with you, senator. We're staying here. Cut the crap!" He squeezed the wrist until it was withdrawn in pain.

"We'll see!" Rubbing the hurt wrist, the senator rushed from the room.

"We're not going out there," Marvina reiterated through her tears. "Now we know that they will try to kill us anywhere."

"I think you're right. It's getting tighter and tighter. We'll make it our way." He grinned at her, and she calmed down, her face becoming determined.

Carpenter took the last bite of his sandwich and a sip of coffee. "That's better," he said, talking to himself aloud. "We'll make it." He stood, uncoiling into a lazy stretch. "She's okay," he said.

Marvina studied him momentarily with concern. At that instant secretaries, aides, and senators began to enter the room. Carpenter went toward the committee chairman. Marvina tagged along.

"Mr. Carpenter, I understand you had some difficulty after this morning's meeting," the senator said, putting down a leather portfolio.

"Yes, sir, that's right."

"It hasn't been easy."

"No, sir, it hasn't. My attorney and I have decided that we'd just as soon not take another chance out there."

"You want to stop giving testimony?"

"I have no objection to that. I just feel . . . we feel that it's too chancy to have it with an audience. I'm sure you understand that anyone out there is in a position to make holes in me."

The senator nodded sagely. He dropped his voice to a confidential tone. "I'm certain that it worries you. You do know, however, the importance of a *public* inquiry."

"We're not going to be targets."

"Believe me, I don't want you to be targets. This is very difficult for all of us. I understand this was explained to you by the committee's counsel. It's a tightrope and we're all on it. Survival depends on a public inquiry."

"I don't give a damn about any survival but ours," Carpenter said, and turned away.

The committee chairman reached out helplessly, touching Carpenter.

Carpenter stared at the hand, picked it off, and said, "I don't like to be touched."

The senator left him and hurried from the room. He returned almost immediately, accompanied by Roose. The two, their heads inches from one another, had drawn faces as they carried on a deep whispered conversation. Their eyes flicked over at Carpenter, and then they continued.

The others in the room seemed to be conscious that some decision was pending, for most of their attention was on the two men.

"Don't compromise," Marvina said.

"I won't."

The senator from Idaho entered the room again, accompanied by Sandy Hair. They looked strangely relaxed. The senator's anxiety had vanished. Both joined the chairman and Roose's discussion. Sandy Hair listened a moment and then turned slightly and spoke directly into Senator Wilby's ear. The senator grinned.

Carpenter felt uneasy watching the four men. All four were enemies, he decided. Perhaps they were different sorts, but enemies just the same. Looking at Marvina, he knew that they were of the same mind. *We*, he thought. He had never shared anything with another person before and it pleased him that he and she were one, a father and a daughter against everyone, against the common threat of the world. He wondered what she would feel if she knew that Fuller . . . He would never tell her. There was no reason for her to know.

Roose left his group and approached Carpenter. His expression was grave. "Dear Christ," he exclaimed in a hiss.

"I'm sorry about the trouble I'm causing," Carpenter said without sincerity.

"A closed hearing is out of the question. That's exactly what they want. Look at the son of a bitch back there. He's as pleased as punch."

"We're not changing our minds," Marvina said.

"Suppose we bring in more cops." Roose stood hunched over, his hands on his hips.

"No deal. I know what they can do. You told us about them, remember."

"If we have everybody searched . . ."

Marvina shook her head. "Who's going to search the searchers? No thanks. There are too many ways around that. I'm willing for us to take some chances, but not stupid ones."

"We're all taking chances," Roose said, looking at Carpenter.

"No," she insisted.

"What the hell will you settle for?"

Carpenter glanced at Roose. "Clear the room and I'll testify. And I want the door locked up."

"How about the press? Can they stay?"

"It depends on which ones."

"There's no damn way for me to know which ones are on our side."

"There's not much point then, is there? There's no way for me to know, either."

"Christ."

"What happened to the guy this morning?"

"Which one?" Roose looked puzzled.

"The one the guard stopped, the one who didn't get away."

"Okay, you made your point." Roose nodded. "We'll have to do it your way. I don't know what good it all will do, but we don't have a choice."

"What happened to him?" Marvina interjected. "The assailant."

"I thought you knew."

"No, I didn't know."

Roose looked back over at the huddled group across the room. "He killed the guard and escaped," he said, nodding a greeting to one of the returning senators as he smiled at the old man.

CHAPTER TWELVE

The large Senate hearing chamber looked huge with only the front tables filled. Sound in it echoed and became more important than the people making it; it was distinct unto itself and seemed to have little connection with human activity.

Carpenter wondered if he had made a mistake in not allowing an audience and the press. He saw among the faces at the senatorial table only one that was pleased with the arrangements. The senator from Idaho had rolled back in his chair, his thin lips curved in pleasure, his eyes sharp little black whips. His sandy-haired friend was massaging his neck. The drunken sleeping senator seemed to be the only one not aware that the rules of the game had changed. He slumbered on.

Roose briefly spoke about the incident of the morning. The description was depressing, and with the exception of the two senators, one sleeping, the other smiling, they all showed fear.

An attempt at assassination within the halls of Congress had its chilling effect; including a quieting of debate each time the senator from Idaho opened his mouth, even if it was to yawn.

"I believe we were talking about Roland Lessy's reaction

to your resignation from the CIA," the committee counsel said.

"Yes, sir."

"Did he, during that reaction, note the reasons that MPI was important to him and the Agency?"

"Obliquely."

"Obliquely? What do you mean?"

"That he had no intention of losing it, that he had made me its chief executive officer because he had trusted my personal loyalty to him, that he would remove me just as easily."

"Did he make an attempt?"

"No, sir. He began to have his own troubles over the Fuller business."

"Were there other proprietaries?"

"Yes, sir. There were many. They were sometimes referred to as the Delaware corporations, many being incorporated there."

"Name some other than your own."

"Caribbean Marine Aero Corporation, Air America, Air Asia, Intermountain Aviation, Southern Air Transport, Pacific Corporation. Over the years there were many more. I've mentioned some that have been previously identified."

The senator from Idaho said, "This is tripe. Let's move to the accusation against Mr. Carpenter."

Roose glanced at the others at the table, his eyes appealing for help. There was none. The chairman stared back momentarily and then nodded to continue.

"Was MPI profitable?"

"I *told* you this was tripe! Don't you listen to me?"

Roose again looked to the chairman. It was a tortured moment.

"The Farbie Building," the chairman said, "does concern us. There is an accusation."

The last small support was gone. Roose swallowed.

"Mr. Carpenter, you've been accused of destroying the Farbie Building. A young lady from the Farbie Institute has testified that she saw you." Roose bowed his head; his voice had a dead quality. "Do you deny this?"

"Yes, sir."

"You realize that this is directly in contradiction to her testimony."

"Yes, sir."

A secretary had entered and gone to Sandy Hair. He rose and left with her.

"Do you realize that a man died as result of the explosions?"

"No, sir. I saw no reference to casualties in the press."

"A Mr. Simons suffered a fatal heart attack."

"That's unfortunate."

Roose spread his fingers out on the table. He seemed to be counting them. Seconds passed. The others at the head table grew restive, uncertain at the silence. The chairman covered his microphone and said a few words to Roose. Roose stood up and stared at Carpenter. "I agree with you, Mr. Carpenter, the death was unfortunate." He glanced at the senator from Idaho. "I'm not convinced it was important. Mr. Simons died of his heart attack two days after the Farbie Building explosion."

The chairman left his chair, too, and went to the counsel, wrapping an arm over his back. Deep in whispered conversation the two began pacing along the back of the room.

Marvina said, "I think it's over."

Carpenter nodded. There was no doubt that the senator from Idaho was controlling the hearing, now that the room had been emptied of public critical response. The other senators wouldn't buck him privately.

During this pause Sandy Hair reentered, appraised the

room's activity, and returned to his task of massaging the senator. He also began talking into the ear of his charge. Wilby showed pleasure.

Not good, Carpenter decided. The safety he had arrived at created a loss, a new sort of threat, one he didn't understand, and that was bad. He had a feeling that, somehow, Roland Lessy was now fully controlling what he wanted within the building and better able to maintain what he wanted outside. He was beginning to fear what the others there seemed to fear. He felt some relief when Roose and the chairman motioned for him to join them.

"Do you think we ought to go?" Marvina asked.

"They're not going to hurt us," he answered.

"I'm not sure," she said. "I'm getting to be like you are, expecting anything at any time."

"We'll chance it." He smiled. They rose and joined the two men.

Roose was grave in tone. "We can give you protection, Mr. Carpenter, after the hearing, if it can be open. There's nothing we can do now. I'm certain you're not blind to what is happening. Everyone here is afraid for his own skin. They know what the stakes are. Roland Lessy is extremely powerful as long as he can operate in the dark and you're giving him that."

"Describe your protection."

"Anything you want, we'll arrange."

"Lessy controls anything you'd call protection."

"We'll go outside government facilities and resources. Anything. It might take a while, but we can put something together."

"There's nothing I trust."

Roose gestured helplessly. "There's no point in going on." He sought confirmation from the chairman and received a weak nod. Roose walked back to his place at the table and packed his briefcase in one motion. He paused as the bell sounded for a Senate vote.

Even the sleeping senator awoke. It was as if an alert had sounded, relieving everyone there of immediate responsibility. It was time to abandon the moment.

Carpenter knew exactly who was being abandoned. The hearing was over for him. He watched as the chamber emptied. Marvina and he would have to survive as best they could.

The chairman returned briefly to his place, banged the gavel, and said, "Until further notice, these proceedings are suspended," and he hurried after the others. There had been no one to hear him, except Carpenter and Marvina.

Perhaps there had never been anyone who could have saved them. He felt vaguely guilty about Roose's last appeal, the patriotic pitch, using the same words as Fuller once had. He put a hand on Marvina's waist and directed her toward the interior Senate chambers. "And look what happened to Fuller," he said aloud.

She glanced back at him, confused and worried by the odd comment.

"We'll make it," he said. There was no one in the interior room and they walked through it.

There was a guard in the hall. He moved forward, saying, "Hey, where did you come from?" and reached for Marvina.

Carpenter caught the arm and slammed it against the wall.

"Hey!" the guard exclaimed.

The excitement was good, the feeling was fresh and clean, nothing of the reasoned perplexity of the hearing where everything was knotted and interlocked.

"How would you like to guide us out of here?" he asked.

"What are you talking about?" The guard was genuinely puzzled.

"Keep your voice down or I'll break your arm."

The man stared into Carpenter's cold eyes and nodded.

"I don't know much about this place, but there must be a parking lot."

"If your name's Carpenter, forget it. There's instructions about you."

"No chance there, then?"

"You haven't got a chance anywhere."

"New guards on duty?"

"Yeah, something like that."

"Visitors have been cleaned out?"

"Hours ago."

"Okay. I'm going to tell you something and I want you to listen. I don't want questions. First, I'm going to tell you that I'll kill you if I don't have your full cooperation. I'll feel sorry about doing it, but I don't have any choices. You have a family. Think about them."

The guard's eyes widened.

"Second. We're going to find another Capitol guard, you and I. I expect you to be friendly and to talk nice to him. Otherwise, you'll both be dead. If everything works out, you'll both live and enjoy your families."

He released the guard's arm and shoved him to the middle of the hall. Keeping a hand lightly on the man's lower back, he told Marvina to stick close, and the three walked briskly.

Turning the next corner, they found two guards rushing toward them. Carpenter's man didn't say a word. He seemed frozen by the unexpected sight. The two neared on the run.

Using his guard's back for cover, Carpenter pulled his gun from his belt and released its safety.

As the two guards came opposite they stopped abruptly. Their weapons looked like cannons. Carpenter fired twice and both men pitched forward, blood spurting across the stone floor.

Shouts echoed along the corridors. Carpenter touched his captive's back. "Where's the nearest empty office?"

"The end of the corridor. I don't think it'll be empty."

"The place has been cleared. Grab that one," he said, pointing to a corpse. "Let's move." They dragged the dead man to the end of the corridor, Marvina collecting the guns, each mounted with a silencer. The office was empty. Carpenter had his guard strip while he did the same to the dead one. Marvina put the smallest uniform on over her clothes and he, the largest. Finding some shears on one of the desks, he cut Marvina's hair, lopping off her longest tresses.

"What I won't do to stay alive," she said.

"They'll know," the guard in his underwear said.

"It's close enough," Carpenter said, circling her as he checked her hair.

Marvina looked down at the loose-fitting jacket and pants.

"It's not the best fit, but it'll do for our purposes." He whirled toward the guard. "What's the closest exit?"

"From here?"

The answer infuriated Carpenter. "You said the wrong thing," he said, and hit the guard on the side of the head. The guard looked surprised, then anguished, then he collapsed.

"He didn't do anything wrong," Marvina said.

"He'll feel better about it later when he finds out he's still alive."

Carpenter suddenly fell silent, motioning for her to do the same. Someone went down the hall outside. He looked down at the smeared trail of blood coming in under the door. He wasn't clear yet. The footsteps hesitated outside. Nothing's easy, he told himself. It was always chancy.

Time and surprise were the only advantages. It was now or never, and the outcome of never was certain. They moved to either side of the door. He opened it, letting it swing wide, loose.

A series of holes appeared on the opposite interior wall, the only sound the dull thuds of impact and broken plaster. With gun ready he dived into the hall, firing. There was only one man, surprised by the assault; he had a joyous triumphant look as he toppled over. Carpenter shot him twice more before he hit the ground.

"Let's go." Carpenter scrambled to his feet and started back in the direction they had come from.

Marvina followed. "Where are we going?"

"The way we came in."

Carpenter and she loped easily, slowed by Marvina's awkward pace in the guard's ill-fitting shoes. She had rolled her own and several of the other guns in his jacket and tucked them under her arm. Carpenter broke light bulbs as they went, leaving the hall behind them shrouded.

They encountered no further opposition though they could hear shouts and calls behind them. Soon they were back in the hearing chamber.

"What are we going to do now?" she asked when he hesitated and looked into the lit room.

"You did well," he said. He had pride in her ability, in her quickness. "Damn well."

"That wasn't my question." She was smiling happily.

He looked back into the hearing room. "We've got to knock those lights out and then go out the front door."

She began to flip wall switches until everything was dark. Then she hammered on the switch until there was a sudden glare of an electric short. She looked demonic in the flare of blue light holding a pistol butt above her head.

"That's it," he said. "Come."

He led her through the dark chamber, moving faster when he found the main aisle up the middle.

"I'm going to hit the door hard," he said, "and then we're going out fast."

The double doors at the end, vaguely outlined by the dim outside light, sprang apart from the lock and swung wide as the pair of them burst through.

There was a surprise. A pair of guards had been standing on the other side, deep in conversation. They both turned and reached for their guns.

"Hold it," Carpenter said, his legs spaced wide, braced to shoot.

They showed no sign of movement. Their faces seemed puzzled as their eyes scanned the two in guard uniforms. "Who the hell are you?" one asked.

"Friends," Carpenter replied, and motioned with his gun for them to move down the hall toward the Capitol entrance.

"What's going on?"

"All of us are done for the day."

"What the hell you talking about?"

The contradiction between the waving gun and the mild tone of the conversation wasn't a problem. The two guards understood the gun as clearly the more dominant of the two themes. The guards began moving, slowly at first.

"Hustle," Carpenter said, and the four of them quickened their pace, closing together, appearing to be four hurrying guards.

When they reached the rotunda, their footsteps clattered and echoed, sounding like those of a squad of soldiers.

A guard at the main entrance watched suspiciously as they approached. A stocky short man, he was obviously more curious than alert. "What's up?" he called out to them.

"It's all over," Carpenter said.

"What's all over?"

"They got them."

"Who got who?"

"Carpenter's dead," Carpenter said.

"That's a relief," the stocky man said, and turned to look outside. Then he said to someone on the steps, "It's all over. They got him."

"And we're going home," Carpenter said, showing the gun as he herded the first two guards out through the entrance and motioned for the new man to join them. Now there were five descending the Capitol stairs.

He made the same gesture to the guard outside. This one seemingly understood instantly and made no objections, joining the pack readily. There was a parked car at the bottom of the steps with two men in street clothes sitting in front and one in the back with a rifle. The man behind the wheel leaned out of the car window to study the gang of approaching guards.

"All over," Carpenter shouted. "Start it up. There's a body coming down."

The man with the rifle looked doubtful. He sat a moment until the other turned the motor over; then he opened the door and got out, leaving the rifle on the seat. "What's the idea?" he said, and then he understood. He whirled back to his seat.

Carpenter fired and the man pitched forward, his legs extended out the car door. The one in front stared at the body for a second. Carpenter opened the front door. "Save your life."

The guards followed Carpenter's simple directions, rolling the dead man out onto the sidewalk, packing themselves into the back seat. The driver got out, stood a moment, and then ran. Carpenter took the wheel, made a U-turn, and crashed through a street barrier. Marvina didn't flinch when there was a sudden burst of gunfire; she held a gun on those in back, moving it slowly from target to potential target, her lips tight, determined.

Carpenter emptied the car of guards when he stopped for a red light. "Thanks," he said as they scattered.

"Well," she said, beaming. "Boy, are we in trouble."

CHAPTER THIRTEEN

"Are we really free?" she asked.

He glanced at her, wondering if he had spoken aloud or if in fact she had begun to read his mind. He waited for her to respond to his own doubts about the degrees of freedom. When she didn't, he said, "No. Not really. We're loose for the moment. In some ways, we're worse off now. Our only advantage is that we have more room to surprise. That's an advantage." But not much, he told himself.

"That's not too much," she said.

He was pleased this time that she seemed to know his thoughts. "It's something," he said.

He stayed where the traffic was heaviest, driving carefully, avoiding any abrupt changes that might cause anyone to notice them. He removed the guard's uniform piece by piece during moments of open road. Marvina helped him remove the blouse and then produced his jacket that she had rolled up with guns. Surprised that she had kept it, he nodded.

"It's not too wrinkled," she said.

"Good. I was worried."

She removed her uniform. He wondered how long it would take her hair to grow out. "I'm sorry about your hair," he said.

She shrugged. "It couldn't be helped." She fingered some

loose ends of the sheared hair. "You think he's right?" she asked.

"Who?"

"The committee counsel, Roose. About Lessy."

"I don't know. He seemed to know."

"That bothered me. I wonder if you could have made a difference."

"I don't know that we would still be alive now. I doubt it."

"Doubt what, that you might have made a difference?"

"That, too. I don't see it as our main problem." From the corner of his eye he saw Marvina make a gesture of impatience. Her hands opened briefly. "But yes. If Lessy has the right people, the right files, he may have grabbed it all off. Think about it—complete records of the most embarrassing and incriminating sort on every industrialist, corporate officer, government official, politician. Even the President. Not to mention the instant sell-outs, loyal and talented who fill this carousel every time a new tenant arrives in the White House. Every one of them is looking to grab a brass ring or the coat of a guy who has grabbed one already. Round and round they go, falling all over one another to get at a piece of it." Carpenter chuckled. "Meanwhile Lessy runs off with the fuses. Except he can't help himself. He has to rub their noses in it. The sadist. He could get away with the whole thing without firing a shot. But he has to see them scared. So now half the Senate must be pissing in their boots and the other half gloating over their good fortune. They deserve each other."

Turning from the line of traffic, he drove four blocks and pulled over to the side. It was a rundown section of Washington, the sidewalks filled with old black women sitting on aluminum summer chairs, all talking good-naturedly with one another until Carpenter and Marvina arrived, and then falling silent, eyeing the car and the couple with suspicion.

"You're sure this is a good place to stop," she said.

"It's the best. They might not trust us around here, but they trust official people less. Roland Lessy hates blacks, so he avoids thinking of them."

"Does he know you know that?"

"He thinks most people think like he does." He switched off the engine and threw Marvina the keys. "Lock up. I'm going to find out where we can eat." He left the car and approached the closest group of women.

"Excuse me. I'd like to find a place where my daughter and I can get something to eat."

"What kina place, mister?" It was the woman who looked oldest who answered. She had swollen legs and began to rub them.

"Anything."

"You want that fancy car of yours?" The others in the group beamed proudly at the elderly speaker.

"For a while. I'm looking to trade it in. I'm not choosy about what I trade it for."

"Do tell!"

"Maybe you can work that out for me while my daughter and I go find something to eat."

"That's bullshit, mister!"

"No bullshit. If the plates are changed and it's given a paint job, it would be a nice trade."

"That's more bullshit."

"Have it your way. Where do my daughter and I go to eat? We'll be there if you change your mind."

He started to walk away, toward Marvina who was waiting for him.

"Two blocks up and turn left. It's a bar, but you can find somethin' to eat."

He nodded back at the woman rubbing her knees.

"What was that about?" Marvina asked. "I gather you trust them."

"We have to. The car's no good to us. They know they have to make a quick decision. A patrol car will spot the car in the next hour or sooner. I'm betting on the hour or they would have decided faster. Those people know when it's due. They have to."

"Why?"

"You grew up out west in a small town. You're just learning. Ghetto people know about cops when they're born."

"Know what?"

"That cops are dangerous."

They turned left. Everyone on the street showed some awareness of them. There were looks and hard stares, even from the children.

"Why did you tell them I was your daughter?" she asked.

"I think of you that way."

A skinny old man with plastered gray hair sat on the curb in front of the bar. A can of beer sat next to him.

Marvina placed her hand in Carpenter's and held hard. "That's nice," she said. "I'm glad you said that even if I'm too old to be anyone's daughter, even my father's."

"I never had a daughter before," he said, and removed his hand to usher her through the open bar door.

It was cloudy dark inside and noisy with gaiety until they entered. Carpenter stepped to the bar, sliding a stool aside. "Looking for some food," he said to the bartender. "I was told we might get some here."

The bartender's dusky face never turned completely toward him. The eyes, however, did, and then looked at the others in the bar. "They's a table in back. You gonna have to take what they is."

Carpenter dug in his pocket and came up with a loose twenty dollar bill and put it on the bar. "Make it two steaks. I'm sure they is some steaks."

"Very funny," the bartender said, his eyes on the bill.

"It's your joke."

"There's some steaks."

"Good. Soon there'll be someone looking for me and my daughter. Send him back to see me."

"What does he look like?"

"You'll recognize him." He paused. "There's another twenty in it if the steaks come real soon. We're in a hurry." He took Marvina's hand and walked through the smoke to the rear. His eyes adjusted rapidly to the dark and he saw a line of suspicious flickering glances.

Carpenter seated himself in the most distant seat so that he could see the entrance.

"What are you staring at?" she asked.

"Hell," he answered, looking at the human shapes outlined in the smoky open doorway.

She turned and nodded.

A small figure scurried into the bar. It hesitated, then plunged on until it reached Carpenter and Marvina.

"You were talking to Mama," it said, bent, jittery, not looking as if it had ever had a "Mama."

"You can make a trade for me?"

"Right."

"What do I get?"

"Shit, man, it runs. What more do you want?"

"That sounds all right. I just want to know what it is?"

"It's out front. Want to take a look?"

"Okay." He rose, telling Marvina that she'd be fine, and followed the small man to the door, where he heard the merits of the ancient rusty half-ton truck.

"One thing," the car dealer said. "The iron you got— they go with the trade?"

"I want one pistol, the rifle in back, and all the ammunition clips. The rest is yours."

"The uniforms?"

"Keep them."

"Sounds okay, then?"

"Fine."

Carpenter and the youth went back into the darkness. When he returned to his table, the steaks had arrived. He asked Marvina for the car keys and then handed them to the boy. "You make the necessary transfer of the goods from the car."

"It'll be ready to go when you're done here."

"How's the gas?"

"Shit, you want everything."

Carpenter pulled out another twenty and put it in his hand. "I'd appreciate it."

"Glad to oblige. I'll leave the keys in the ignition." He turned and boldly sauntered away.

"We're all set, daughter," he said to Marvina.

She reached across the small table and patted one of his hands and smiled contentedly.

Carpenter stowed the rifle behind the bench seat in the cab, gathered up the loose clips of ammunition, and filled his pockets. Marvina took the extra pistol and after receiving some quick instructions on its operation, she put it under her dress, in front so that her belly bulged. "The metal's cold," she said.

The truck ran smoothly, its motor rough only at street speeds. It hummed when they hit the highway into Maryland. It was after nine, the sky's heavy warm gray blanket had thickened when Carpenter pulled by a roadside phone booth at a rest stop. He searched for change in a pocket and called his private number at MPI.

"Any messages?" he asked.

There was a moment of hesitation from his operator. Then, "Who's this?"

"Who the hell would it be?"

"Mr. Carpenter? I . . . I was told that you were no longer with us."

"Who told you?"

"Mr. Sofer. He was elevated today to chairman of the board. He said you wouldn't be calling in again."

"I guess he's right." Carpenter hung up. He dialed the White House. "Sy Basset, please."

"One moment, please."

He hung up and dialed Basset's home number. Mrs. Basset answered. "May I talk to Sy?"

"I'm sorry but he's not home."

"Damn. I thought he would be home already. I needed some information that I know he has. Oh, dear. He has a Congressional Directory there, doesn't he?"

"I think so. Who's this?"

"Stevens. Wally Stevens. How do you do?"

"Have we met?"

"I don't think so."

"Your voice is familiar."

"It would be a big favor if you'd look up something for me. You'd have my everlasting thanks."

"I suppose I could look it up."

"That's great. I wouldn't ask but I'm not in my office and . . . I need two addresses. The senator from Idaho, Wilby, and another for his head assistant."

"Wilby. I know his address. We were just at his home two weeks ago."

"You probably know his aide, a sandy-haired young guy."

"Goodness, I know who you mean. He's not on the senator's staff. It seems like it, though, doesn't it?"

"Yes, it does. I thought he was for sure."

"That's Hinsey. Bob Hinsey. He has an apartment at Watergate."

"Then all I need is the Wilby address."

She gave it to him, and he thanked her.

After climbing back into the truck, he sat thoughtfully, staring at a highway police cruiser circling the rest area.

"Did you call a friend?"

He turned and stared at her. "No." He watched the cruiser loop about slowly at the far end of the area, then he steered the truck out and onto the highway. At his first opportunity he took a turnoff, over a highway bridge, and then got back on the road to Washington.

It began. As his forehead beaded with sweat, he sensed that the attack was coming faster than normal. He pulled off on the apron. "You'll have to drive for a while."

She searched his face and didn't move.

"Hurry," he said. "I don't dare get out."

She climbed out and went around. By the time she seated herself behind the wheel, he found his hold weakening. Wedged back against the door, he searched frantically for his pills, finding it incredible that he couldn't feel them anywhere, in any pocket.

"What are you looking for?"

"Pills," he gasped. "They must have fallen out."

Oh, God, it was cold. The rain was so hard; he couldn't remember it ever having poured so heavily. He was soaked and shivering. And the darkness was impossible. There was nothing visible. His eyes should have adjusted by now; there had to be some light somewhere. He looked up and couldn't see above the jungle foliage. Now it was hot. He wondered why he had felt cold. It hadn't made sense.

At least they wouldn't follow in this. If he couldn't see, they couldn't either. But he had to hurry. He could be in the mountains before they caught up and he might be able to lose them entirely. The jungle floor was a resisting bog, juicing up and holding each foot as he moved. Each step seemed to take minutes. And the fucking leeches were draining his strength.

He tripped and fell, wallowing in the morass, slowly regaining his feet, wondering if he would be able to move again, stumbling forward, falling, lying there, thinking he might never rise, that it no longer mattered if he did.

Then he knew that they were with him, their feet sucking into the swamp, moving relentlessly around him. How could they see him? He knew they did. They were watching him. Why didn't they kill him? He had killed so many of them. They were an army of children with beardless innocent yellow faces. They never stopped.

CHAPTER FOURTEEN

The ferocious cold made his bones rattle. He sensed that no one wanted him on the plane, that no one understood why he was there. That was all right with him. He didn't want to be there. The lousy fucks kept asking him questions. How the hell did he know? He'd find out, but he would never tell them, he'd never tell them shit. Who the hell were all these bastards? Grabbling like a bunch of monkeys, talking gibberish. Where had they come from? What were they doing with him?

He studied the shiny-faced, glowing kid in the starched shirt who had sat next to him with the clipboard.

"I just need a few quick answers. There's been a decision made to take you off at Guam. I just want to be positive who you are. The name given us doesn't make any sense. Say something. Anything. You're among friends again. I don't know what you know or what you want to know. Did you forget how to speak?" The man's eyes furtively skipped around the plane and then back. "Do you remember Roland Lessy?"

I'm not stupid, he said without sound or moving his lips. You are, you stupid shit, if you think I'm going to say anything.

"I can't tell what you know. I don't know if you know who everybody else is, here on board. They don't know who you are. They don't know where you came from.

Well, no matter. We'll find out. I'm betting that you are Carpenter, that somehow you made it. In case it means anything to you, the others here are flyboy POWs, on their way home. Richard Nixon is President of the United States.

"Are you cold? Your teeth are chattering. I'll get you another blanket."

He turned and looked out the window. God it was cold. It's been a long time to stay cold.

He opened his eyes and shivered from the blast of air coming from the open window. It was night. There was no plane and the puffy sunlit clouds were gone. He rolled his head to see Marvina driving, tears washing her gleaming cheeks.

"How long have I been out?" he asked.

"Oh, God! Oh, dear God!" She pulled the truck to the side of the road and thrust herself at him, embracing him, suffocating, crying, loosing wild sounds of relief.

He finally pushed her back, feeling a mixture of reluctance and relief when he finally succeeded. No one had ever shown such emotion; he had never felt anything similar before. "Where are we?"

She was about to launch herself at him again. He held her back. "Answer me, damn it." He looked at his watch and caught the light from a passing car. It was almost four in the morning.

"I'm not sure," she said, feeling his cheeks.

"Were we driving the whole time?"

"Yes."

"Still Maryland?"

"No."

"Virginia?"

"I . . . think . . . so."

"There was nothing else for you to do. You did okay. Stop looking so worried. It'll be a while before I completely recover. But I'm coming around. I'm already feeling stronger. It's nothing to worry about. How far are we from Washington?"

"An hour, maybe a little longer."

"Not bad. Turn around and head back."

"You want me to drive?"

"Yeah, why not?" He smiled. "We'll have to get rid of the truck. You drive and I'll look for a car so we can make a switch. That all right with you, daughter?"

They stole a car from an apartment complex near Mount Vernon, Carpenter jumping the wires. Later, nearer Washington, he switched its plates with a car parked in a one-car garage.

Dawn was breaking as they reached the city limits.

"I don't understand what we're doing here again," she said.

"Where did you think we'd go?"

She looked reflectively at the road. "I thought we'd be running."

"Where to?"

"Somewhere, away from here."

"They expect that. It's easier to be picked off running. I don't like running. There are a few things we can do here."

"Like what?"

It was a simple direct challenge. He glanced at her; she was expecting an answer, any answer. He had none; he didn't really know. He measured the feelings he had about the alternatives that were possible.

"We're going to find Lessy," he said. "He'll understand that we're even now. I've just got to tell him that we're even. Maybe it'll be over, then."

She looked at him incredulously and finally turned away. "Are you sure? Think about it."

Maybe she was right, he thought. Lessy might not accept that they were even, that Fuller had been paid for. And maybe there was no way to come out even unless he killed Lessy. That had to be thought about.

"You don't know where to find him," she said. Her voice was a monotone, her sentence a plain fact.

"Not yet."

He turned toward northeast and stopped in a supermarket parking area. "We're going to take our chances in losing the car," he said. She didn't respond. "We're going to hole up for the day and get some sleep."

She looked at the surrounding area. She didn't seem impressed. The somber buildings were just a shade darker than the sky. She adjusted the pistol sitting on her stomach and waited until Carpenter moved.

The streets were empty except for a few cars and several sleepy workmen. The hallway of the apartment house had a dirty marble veneer that had been washed with a muddy mop. Carpenter pushed one of the bells. There was no answer. He finally opened the front door, using a piece of plastic. He motioned for Marvina to follow.

On the third floor he studied a sign on the door he wanted.

"What does it say?" Marvina asked.

"Nothing," he said, taking the piece of paper and crumpling it.

"Who lives here?"

"A girl." As he looked at the door, he paused. Briefly he considered leaving. There was something about the note that disquieted him. There was no hint of trouble about it. It was simple. Just "Out. L."

"What's her name?"

"Liz, I think.'"

"A friend? A girl friend?"

"No. She was safe." He remembered how skinny she was, how anxious to please. Sofer had said Lessy knew about her? He told himself that he had been too careful. It was always important to be careful. Maybe he hadn't been careful enough.

"Why are we standing here?"

He paid no attention to her question.

Out. L.

That was a strange note for someone who thought and talked in long emotional terms. It was one reason he liked going to see her. There was a bluntness about her, but it wasn't terse. Lessy wouldn't know about that. He tried the doorknob. When it worked and the door opened, he held it without pushing it further. Then he smelled the odor and closed the door again.

Marvina said, "Whew. That's awful."

He looked unwell. "You stay out here a minute. I'll be back." He reopened the door and entered.

He knew the smell. Not new death but old death—rotting death. The wash of early morning gave the small apartment a coziness, an odd security. He went through the small rooms and found her, a rigid naked corpse tied to a chair in the living room, the cords embedded in her swollen flesh. She wasn't skinny any more. He wanted to scream. They had pulled her nails, burned her breasts, hurt her eyes. She didn't know anything and couldn't find peace by telling them. They hadn't believed her.

He and Lessy were not even. They would never be until Lessy was dead.

After opening windows, covering the girl with a blanket, and closing the living room door, he returned for Marvina and brought her in.

"What happened in here?" she asked.

"The smell will clear in a while. You take the bedroom

and get some sleep. Close the door. The open window will make it clear soon."

She paused and studied the closed living room door, then fled into the bedroom.

Carpenter squatted with his back against the outside door and stared sightlessly into the apartment. He saw Liz, the image of her tormented body on the other side of the closed door. It wouldn't vanish, it persisted in its horror. His eyes became wet as he tried to remember the way she had been before and he couldn't. He knew that he would never again be able to reconstruct a picture of her as she had been. He tightened his eyelids as the tears began.

Accustomed to horror, he had never before seen such an extreme. He tried to imagine how it might have happened, for even Lessy had never seemed capable of such cruelty. Why had they put out her eyes?

Liz must have died long before whoever it was had finished. Someone had desecrated her body with wanton ruthlessness. It was an act of vengeance, a random monstrousness that informed Carpenter he could expect nothing less. Whatever the game was, it was total.

Carpenter heard Marvina moving restlessly. He opened his eyes and saw her standing at the threshold.

"I'm worried about you," she said.

"Don't worry."

"You've been crying."

"I'll be all right. I must be tired."

"It's more than that, isn't it?"

He paused, confused about how to answer. "We've got to find Lessy."

"You really think that you can make peace with him?"

"I don't think that any more."

"Then what's the point?"

"There's a point. Go back to bed. You'll need your sleep. We both do."

She left.

He could hear her sitting on the bed, the springs groaning. Finally he heard her lie down. Soon the apartment was quiet. He closed his eyes again.

CHAPTER FIFTEEN

The Watergate was out. Its very complexity meant time wasted. Sandy Hair was safe as long as he stuck to its confines. So there wasn't a choice. They had to work on the senator from Idaho at the plush Foxhall Road address and pray for some luck.

The first look at Senator Wilby's house gave Carpenter the feeling that he was dealing with a situation that was clearly better than fifty percent in his favor. It was a large Tudor house sitting on substantial grounds loaded with shrubs and outbuildings surrounded by a tall wire fence. There was a large servant population and much activity. One disadvantage was a dog kennel full of Dobermans. Presumably these were released at night to patrol the grounds when the house bedded for the night.

There were two main houses on opposite sides of the senator's estate. The eastern house was dark, empty even of staff. A heavy building of pinkish stucco, it looked more mausoleum than living quarters. So it interested Carpenter, even though it was quite far from the senator's home, across five hundred feet. Between them and the compound fence was open lawn that plunged downward in a deep slope.

Afterward they had dinner in a truck stop cafe over the Maryland border. Marvina was reflective, staring at the plate in front of her, glancing every now and then at Carpenter as he leafed through all the daily papers and picked at his food. He finally folded the paper and piled it on the seat next to him.

"Nothing," he said. He raised his head. "There's an item on me, saying that a witness identified me as the person who blew up the Farbie Building. Nothing, absolutely nothing about an assassination attempt or any trouble in the Capitol."

He drank the steamy black coffee in a few gulps.

"I don't know if I can accept that someone wants me dead," Marvina said. "It seems so unreal."

He saw Liz again. He felt anger, a flush of it burning in his brain, like the hot coffee in his throat. He wondered when Liz had realized that she was going to die. She probably never did. "Are you finished?" he asked.

"Finished thinking or eating?"

"I meant, eating. It's getting dark out."

"I can't believe it. I can't believe that someone wants to kill me."

He rose and collected the check. "I'll see you outside," he said. He left the table and paid the woman at the cash register and went into the open air. Marvina's problem with the reality of the past few days would pass, he told himself. Her present attempt at analysis was the natural course for most human beings brought up with a sense of innocence. It wasn't stupidity that she was contending with; it was comparison. Her mind was shielding her from the raw truth.

She joined him in the car. He pumped the gas pedal and then twisted the loose wires together. The motor started immediately. He was pleased that he had not stolen a lemon.

"I called my secretary," she said.

He waited.

"I don't have any more doubts," she said.

"What did she say? Your secretary."

"She didn't say anything. Her mother answered the phone. She was crying. My secretary is dead." She stared at Carpenter.

"That's it?"

"No."

"What happened?"

"The first night we were trying to stay alive, two men went to her house and began asking questions about me. They wanted to know where I was. She didn't know, but they wouldn't believe her." Marvina didn't finish. She sat silently looking ahead at the road.

He could guess the rest. It had been a busy night for Lessy's people. Undoubtedly they worked for a proprietary agency, on contract, supposedly a private detective agency. He wondered what Marvina's reaction would be if he told her about it. Fuller wouldn't believe it at first, finally reacting against Carpenter's acceptance of it as a necessity for national security: "You're mad," he had said, "completely mad. The only reason I told you was so that we could have a laugh at some of the crazy things Lessy keeps coming up with. And you didn't think it's funny, you think it's a good idea. You're crazier than Lessy!"

Marvina broke in. "You know the rest, don't you. You know what happened."

He nodded.

The oncoming car lights took his concentration as they headed back into Washington.

He took the rifle with him. It had limited use because its only ammunition was in it, but it had protective advantages because of its telescopic sight and range. The stucco house was alarm wired against a break-in, making an obvious entrance difficult.

After a quick examination of the outside he returned to Marvina and sat down on the grass next to her. They were two shadows, barely visible to one another, and they spoke in whispers.

"That didn't take long."

"It never does," he said.

"Why do you need this house?"

"We need a base and some of the material inside. It's just outside the fence and useful. That's one of the problems we have, the need to improvise."

"Can you get inside?"

"I think so. I have one little chore so that I can get by the security alarm system."

"I thought that was what burglar alarms were all about, to prevent that."

"Most people think so. That makes it easier."

"Are you going to do it now?"

"In a few minutes. I want to listen to the senator's dogs for a while." He hunched forward on his knees and closed his eyes. He could hear Marvina breathing lightly and finally managed to ignore it as he listened.

A dinner party was on in the senator's house. There was a peal of distant laughter and the sounds of staff moving, glasses tinkling, dishes. The dogs were comparatively quiet. Every now and then one would bark, the others joining in briefly, and then they would fall silent. Usually a sound coming from the house would set them off. They were nervous animals, Carpenter judged. But they weren't as bad as they might have been, he decided. They didn't always react.

He opened his eyes and stood up, then motioned for Marvina to join him as he went down the long lawn to the fence. On the way he collected small stones as he went. "How's your throwing arm?" he asked.

"I don't know."

"The kennels are not too far."

When he reached the fence, he threw a stone at the low-lying complex of kennels. At first there was a growl and then a series of yips, then a burst of barking. When it was silent again, he threw another stone and the pattern was repeated.

"What are you doing?" she asked.

"I want the people in the house to get used to the dogs barking. After a while it won't mean anything to them."

Another stone, more barking.

He continued until the barking became constant. He gave Marvina his small collection of stones. "Now you do it."

She looked at the stones doubtfully. It took her three throws before she achieved the same results.

"I'll be back," he said, and left her. At a slow trot he returned to the house and circled it until he found the outdoor tool shed. Along with a riding mower, there was a broad assortment of gardening and work tools. He picked up a sledgehammer. Returning to the house, he felt along the stucco finish until he found a broad area widely separated by windows. He put the rifle on the ground and took a step back from the blank wall.

Heaving the sledge back for momentum, he brought it forward heavily against the surface of the house. He listened to its dull thud as it broke through on the first blow. With the dogs barking, it didn't make any extraordinary noise. He was pleased with the brittleness of the stucco as it fell in large hunks.

The crackings of the wood inside the walls were some concern. As the plywood splintered open, the cracks were as sharp as explosives going off. The framework timbers sagged and collapsed. He had an enormous hole, larger than he had planned.

The dogs were yelping excitedly. Someone at the senator's house shouted, "The Goddamned dogs! There must be a bitch in heat somewhere!" Then it was quiet except for the dogs. Carpenter smiled.

He walked into the house through the blackness. Gray shapes covered with dust cloths loomed in the dark like cartoon ghosts. He slipped past swiftly and, finding a staircase, he flung himself upstairs. He had expected to find the switch to the burglar alarm in the master bedroom. It wasn't there. Searching one room at a time, he unexpectedly found it in the kitchen, and turned it off. As far as he could see, the owner had not installed a backup system, satisfied no doubt that windows and doors were the fundamental break-in areas.

Carpenter went out and got Marvina.

"What an awful mess," she said as she followed him through the hole.

The dogs were still barking.

She said, "I thought I heard thunder but I guess it was just you."

The next step was gathering a telephone and every bit of telephone wire. Carpenter took every hookup apart, tearing the wire from its wall connector plug and then from the phone. There were six phones in the house and the wire from all of them amounted to more than fifty feet.

"Just about enough," he said happily.

"For what?"

"To tap the senator's calls."

She watched as he spliced the pieces together and hooked them to the lead on one phone. "It looks simple so far," she said.

"It is."

The dogs were quieting; the fierce angry calls from the main house died away. One dog was howling. Carpenter looked off, listening. "We're going to have to annoy them some more." He grinned.

"I'll go," she said.

"You're a good daughter," he said. There was something comforting about being able to use the word *daughter*. They had come a long way in a few days. Fuller didn't have any part in their relationship anymore. The hostile feelings he had had about Fuller had changed. Owen was like someone who had introduced a long-lost father to his child. He was glad he had cut her hair.

He went back to the wire, rolling it into a long loop that he put over his shoulder.

The dogs began again. There was a yelp of pain or surprise. She had probably hit one.

Would Marvina continue as a companion, playing daughter to his role as father? He shook himself, realizing that he was thinking unrealistically. There was too much to be done before he could even contemplate the future.

He checked the wire, making sure the contacts were tight. Lessy first, he told himself.

With Marvina stationed below in the darkness, he hooked his legs around the telephone pole. He wished he had more light than the glazed night sky afforded. He didn't want to make any mistakes, like accidentally touching one of the high voltage wires. That would end it, tossing him straight down. No matter. He wouldn't make a mistake; he wouldn't do that to Marvina.

A car came up the road and he could feel the air move aside as it swooshed past below him. The moment of light it gave showed him the telephone contact box. He removed the cover and let it drop below, then waited for his eyes to readjust to the darkness. It might take him hours to find the right contacts. His body ached with the thought. He connected his wires to a set of screws and scrambled down the pole and joined Marvina.

"Is that it?"

"No." He uncradled the phone and squinted at the dial. He dialed Senator Wilby's number. He dialed it and listened to it ring. He hung up.

"Not right?"

"Not right. When I'm hooked into his line, we'll get a busy signal." He reclimbed the pole and shifted the contacts.

On the third try he received a busy signal. He touched Marvina and made a V with his fingers. Taking the phone back from the road as far as it would reach, he wrapped it in his jacket to deaden its ring.

A long three quarters of an hour went by before it buzzed beneath the cloth.

"Yes, sir. Senator Wilby's residence."

Carpenter was listening.

"May I speak with the senator, please."

"Who shall I say is calling?"

"Tell him Stylup."

"Yes, sir. One moment, sir. I'll see if he can speak to you."

There was dead space. The dinner party at the senator's house jangled in the background with laughter and humming voices.

"Mr. Stylup?"

"Yeah."

"The senator will be with you shortly. He's taking your call in the study."

"Thanks."

The background noise continued for a few minutes. Then the senator came on the line and the butler hung up the first phone.

"What the hell is it, Stylup?"

"Sorry to bother you, senator."

"Just spit it out, boy."

"There's nothing new. Hinsey says it's just a matter of time. He doesn't like for it to drag on, but it'll take another day at least, he says. He thought you'd like to keep on top of it."

"Tell him I appreciate that."

"He's keeping close contact on it. It's a very tight operation. Incidentally, I was told that you have the votes. Any time you want to move, you can have it. . . . The President, as usual, is going along. Basset says there's no problem."

"I'd like to meet with him."

"The President or Basset?"

"Why the hell would I want to meet with those damn fools?"

"I thought . . ."

"Shit, Stylup, I've got to make a decision. They're not going to help."

"Well, I'll talk to Hinsey."

"I'd appreciate that, son. You tell him that I've gone along with this up to now, but I would like a meeting before I make a final decision. When Hinsey knows if it's possible, have him call me."

"I don't know whether you'll get a quick answer, sir."

"Have him call me anyway . . . in an hour."

"I'll tell him."

"You do that, boy. You do that."

The senator hung up. So did Carpenter.

Marvina stirred restlessly, waiting while he mulled over the pieces he now had. "Anything?" she asked.

"Yes and no. That was from someone named Stylup. I never heard of him."

"What did he want?"

"It's not entirely clear. Some of it might have been about us. If it was, they've lost us."

"Good."

"Most of it was about some decision the senator needs to make. He wants to meet with someone. It's also not clear who with."

"Not very helpful."

"Could be. Stylup is calling back in an hour."

CHAPTER SIXTEEN

The hour passed slowly. Mosquitoes had arrived in numbers to torment them, and the evening turned chilly. The two sat close together. Marvina left once to make the long trip to throw stones at the dogs. The phone rang while she was gone. The senator was upset by it.

"Marjorie, I've pleaded with you and now I'm ordering you: Don't *ever* call me at home, ya hear?"

"I was lonely," a sweet voice said.

"Watch television."

"You're havin' a party, aren't you?"

"A party? Where did you get that idea?"

"It sounds to me like a party."

"That's the servants. I was in my study, doing work in my study."

"Where's your little wife?"

"I told you, Marjorie, I don't want you to mention my wife. She's my business."

"Where is she?"

"She went to bed hours ago."

"I don't believe you, honey."

"You better believe me. I'm not going to have this, do you hear? What the hell is going on with you, girl? There's a place for everything. And you got no right to carry on so."

"I was lonely."

"Now, Marjorie, I know it gets lonesome out there, but you got to forbear, do you hear? I had to learn that; you've got to learn that."

"Can't you come into town tonight?"

"God o'mighty, girl, this isn't Thursday!"

"I'm lonely."

"I'm getting mighty angry with you. This is getting to be a poor habit of yours. You don't call me at home. You damn well don't call me." The senator hung up.

Carpenter was amused.

The dogs were viciously yelping, leaping against their kennel barriers.

Marvina returned. "I think some people are leaving the senator's house. The dogs started up by themselves." She sat down next to him. "Anything?"

"The senator has a girl friend on the side. He doesn't like to be called at home."

Headlights shone suddenly at the senator's place and pierced the thick air as they swept the darkness. He and Marvina bent together, lowering their heads, as the first departing vehicle drove by.

There were two more calls. The senator wouldn't speak to either caller, asking instead that they reach him during the day at his office.

Stylup was late. The hour was gone. Carpenter worried that the senator had placed the call himself rather than wait. There was no way of knowing if a call originated from the house. Other guests were leaving.

The last car pulled to the side of the road ten feet away and turned out its lights. The couple in the car silently groped at each other in a series of passionate, if awkward, embraces. Then suddenly they left the car and disappeared into high grass near them. Nothing was spoken, a seemingly unified motive driving them. There was a rustling and movement of tall roadside weeds and a litany of erotic noises and words.

The telephone buzzed beneath the coat.

"What the hell's that?" the male voice asked in panic.

"Oh, Christ!" the woman said.

Both ran for the car.

Carpenter waited until they had gone before picking up the receiver, not wanting the motor sound to escape into it. The ringing had stopped earlier. He hoped he had not missed much and that they wouldn't hear the click.

"What was that?"

"Don't worry. I had my phone checked for taps two days ago. It's been on the fritz this evening. It kept ringing and no one was on it. The phone company is checking it out. Hey, can I see him or not?"

"He doesn't like the idea."

It wasn't Stylup, Carpenter thought. It had to be sandy-haired Bob Hinsey.

"You still worried about the phone? If it'll make you feel any better, I'll check the extensions to make sure no one is listening in. But you don't have a thing to worry about. The servants are safe and I have a very loyal wife. Hold on."

Carpenter listened and for the first time picked up sounds from the caller's end. There was a distant even hum and a subdued gentle swoosh. That wasn't much to go on.

The senator came back on. "Clear, absolutely clear. I can tell you one thing, Bob. I'm not going through with my end unless I get to see him first. I don't get pushed around unless it's to my advantage. You're dealing with the United States Senate, boy, not the White House. I want to sit across from him and get commitments."

"I'm sorry, senator. He doesn't find it necessary. You know me, I'm on your side. My advice is that you either go along or you might be forgotten. He had to move a lot faster than he originally expected but it's all pulled together. If you don't get aboard now, you'll find you missed the boat."

"Don't give me horseshit. He needs me."

"I'm sorry, senator. He's very firm. You know him—when he makes up his mind, you don't unmake it. I wish I could say something different. I really do. I'm looking at him right now and believe me, senator, there's no changing his mind. I don't want to ask him again."

"Tell him what I said."

"It's a mistake. Believe me. Have I ever misled you?"

"Tell him."

"It's a mistake. I'll tell him you insist. But I want you to reconsider before I do. You know what happened to Kulbers today after it was clear that he was responsible for sending those files over to the Farbie Institute."

"I don't give a Goddamn about Kulbers. He was a clerk. I'm a United States Senator."

"I want you to know, sir, that, at this moment, the President of the United States is bringing him a drink."

There was a pause.

"You understand what I'm trying to say to you, senator?" Hinsey added.

Another pause. Carpenter listened to the background hum. They were engine sounds, a smooth reciprocating piston engine.

"No," the senator said.

"I never thought of you as a stupid man. I guess you've been running things your way too long. I'm trying to tell you that you don't run things any more. He does."

"I want to speak to him . . . now."

"You are stupid, senator. He's not going to speak to you now or later."

"You Goddamn *puppy!* You do as I told you. I own you."

"Owned, senator. Just be careful. That's my last bit of friendly advice."

"That's a threat, Hinsey. I can recognize a threat. I don't take threats from ass kissers."

"I'm losing patience."

"Don't give me that bullshit. Once an ass kisser, always an ass kisser. You put him on the line and I'll talk to him directly. I don't talk to ass kissers."

"You're a dead man, senator. You won't live till morning. That's not a threat. It's the truth."

The line went dead.

The senator began clicking his phone as if the line had been cut by error and that an operator could reestablish the connection. He began to shout: "You fucking ass kisser! You cocksucker!" The line became a dial tone.

Carpenter hung up. He stared at Marvina for a second. He was up and running before she had a chance to ask anything. She chased after him. "Where are we going?" she panted.

"The dogs. I've got to get to them before they're released."

"Why?"

He was beyond her hearing. He could hear the barking; they were not yet released. Flying down the slope toward the fence, he gained momentum. He didn't slow, but twisted in the air just before hitting the meshed wire. All of his accelerated weight plunged against it. It held him for an instant, then collapsed. He rolled over and was on his feet speeding toward the kennels. The side of his shoulder was in sharp pain and it radiated down his side as he continued his run. He fell once and quickly sprang to his feet.

He arrived just as the caretaker was reaching for the bolt that opened the side of the kennel, the snarling dogs leaping in readiness. Carpenter dived for the caretaker and just caught his legs, heaving him down hard. The man scrambled for freedom. Carpenter had a leg and brought him down again, then crammed the man's mouth with dirt, and, while he gagged, clubbed him unconscious. Examining the kennel bolt, he took a shovel and twisted the latch so that it couldn't open.

He looked back and saw Marvina stepping through the broken fence. *We*, he thought, and waited. She was carrying his jacket in one hand and her pistol in the other. "I pulled the wire down," she said. "I had a feeling that you didn't need the phone any more."

"I'm going to see the senator. I heard all I needed."

"See him? Why? He's dangerous to us."

"I think he might help us, just to save his own skin."

"What do you want me to do?"

"Stay here and watch that there are no surprises from the outside. Someone might show up to do the job on the senator. I don't want to go with him."

"You're serious."

"I'm serious."

He left her and headed for the senator's house. He didn't expect any difficulty. The house was still open; he could see servants moving about. As he climbed the front steps, he put his jacket on and straightened it.

He walked in and smiled at a startled maid who looked up from her chore of collecting glasses.

"Is the senator still in his study?"

The maid dropped a handful of glasses and fled. When he heard hasty footfalls, he dodged to the wall next to the open door through which the sound was entering. It was funny to see a butler with a shotgun.

He took the shotgun away.

"Tell me where I can find the senator and I'll save his stupid life for him. I'm not here to kill him. I'm here to help him."

The butler seemed doubtful.

Some other person charged from a doorway. Carpenter tripped the second man, who sprawled, slid the length of the waxy floor, and collided with the edge of the fireplace. He didn't rise.

"Is there another one?" Carpenter asked. "If there is, you better call him off. Someone will get really hurt."

The butler went to the door. "Prescott, it's under control," he said. "You won't be needed."

"Good," Carpenter said. "And the senator. May I see him, please."

The butler dipped slightly, as though not ready to fully bow. Carpenter followed him into the recesses of the house.

Senator Wilby had lost his usual ruddy color. He sat at his desk, his body rigid, and peered fearfully at his butler and Carpenter. He seemed about to speak, his jawline quivering.

Carpenter said, "It looks like I'm going to have to save your life as well as my own."

The senator didn't seem grateful.

"I listened to your conversation with Hinsey. You know he means what he says, don't you?"

The senator nodded. The bloat of good food, wine, and liquor dropped from his face leaving the bland heavy flesh wrinkled and loose.

"The first thing we do is get out of here. Agreed?"

The senator neither nodded nor shook his head.

"Whether you like it or not, you're going with me and you'll cooperate. Believe me, I know Lessy. You haven't a chance without me. So rise, senator, and face the world. We have a trip to make."

The senator stood.

Carpenter said to the butler, "I want you to get the senator's limousine out front. We're going to need it. I think you're the one to do the driving."

The butler vanished as Carpenter leaned across the desk and took the senator's arm, pulling him forward.

"I'll tell you something. You might die anyway if you're not one hundred percent helpful. I have a good idea where Lessy is. I'd like your opinion."

"You're hurting my arm."

"He's on the presidential yacht. Am I right?"

"There is no presidential yacht. Carter got rid of it."

"Don't give me the public relations crap. You and I know there's now a new one, no matter what you call it. A bigger one." He tightened his grip on the arm.

"He's on the yacht."

The senator accompanied Carpenter, but his reluctance remained and he required constant prodding in the small of his back. Marvina joined them at the front of the house when the limousine drew up. She was staring distrustfully at the senator. "He doesn't seem agreeable," she said.

"You should understand what he's going through," Carpenter explained. "He doesn't yet fully accept that Lessy would want to kill him. He thinks of us as his major threat."

"Do we need him?"

"Yes."

Listening to this conversation, Wilby seemed comforted. He entered the car without urging.

Carpenter held the door for Marvina. "Keep watch on him," he cautioned. "I'm going back to the other house to get the rifle. We'll need it."

When he returned to the car, he shoved the rifle under their feet in back and jumped in with the others. "Everything but a picnic lunch," he said.

The senator wasn't amused. He looked down at the rifle and moved deeper into the corner as if he were a passenger sharing first class with lepers.

Marvina said, "He called us traitors to this great land of ours."

"I'm beginning to think his old pal Hinsey is right. He's stupid."

The butler looked back and grinned. "Where would you like me to drive, sir?" he asked Carpenter.

"There's a boathouse on the Virginia side of the Potomac. It rents power boats. Do you think you can find it?"

"I think so, sir."

"That's where we're going."

CHAPTER SEVENTEEN

Carpenter found it unsettling to discover that a gray sedan had begun following them on Canal Road. It just appeared and held the same constant speed four car lengths behind. At that hour of the night any and all traffic was suspect. He regarded it as doubtful that another vehicle would coincidentally be taking exactly the same route. It wasn't possible to draw an accurate conclusion immediately. He'd wait to see how long the coincidence lasted and whether there would be a switch made, a replacement by another car with another high radio antenna. He thought it a trifle too soon for them to have sent a check on the senator, especially one that would pick him up a distance from the house.

Being on the jump seat in the back gave him the opportunity to watch both the car and the senator by looking back at Marvina. The senator had not shown any awareness of being followed, or any anticipation of it.

"I find it incredible to think how naive I was," Marvina said. "God, what must my parents be thinking?"

That was painful. He felt as if he had been removed suddenly, that they had not shared the past few days. He wondered how Fuller would have felt to lose fatherhood in a remark. It wasn't important, he told himself, but it remained.

"My father could never have handled it," she continued. "My mother could. She'd adjust to anything. My father couldn't. If he found that everything he believed in was wrong, he would have collapsed and suffered terribly. He wouldn't do anything about it, but he'd never be the same."

He wished he could quiet her. "I'm your father," he said.

She turned and studied Carpenter. "In a way, I guess you are," she said and smiled.

It wasn't what he needed.

The sedan left. A station wagon replaced it. It, too, had a radio antenna.

The senator was throwing glances at both of them as if he had just awakened and was beginning to understand his companions. Carpenter tensed as he watched the senator's eyes. It was clear that a trap was in the making.

"Are you two related?" the senator asked.

"No, of course not," Marvina said.

"There's a resemblance," the senator added.

Marvina laughed.

Carpenter leaned forward and told the butler to change his route, to swing west away from the Potomac.

"Yes, sir."

No surprise. The station wagon stayed on its road.

The senator was looking out his own window and seemed to be watching the wagon's lights until they were swallowed by the terrain.

Soon there was another car with a radio antenna on its roof. This one had two men in it, while the others had had only one.

"Senator," Carpenter asked, "do you have any idea where the yacht is?"

"It was on the Chesapeake. A big place."

"I didn't want to know where it was. I want to know where it is."

The senator looked fearful again.

"Tomorrow is a big day for Lessy, isn't it."

"This is your little party." The senator was sullen.

"If you think they'll change their minds about you once they have Marvina and me, forget it. If you have any intelligence left, you'll cooperate with me."

The senator closed his eyes.

"I might just kill you if I don't feel that I have your wholehearted cooperation."

The senator opened his eyes and studied Carpenter.

"I have nothing to lose," Carpenter said.

"They're on the Potomac," the senator said, and looked away.

"How close to Washington?"

"It's a big river."

"Cooperate, senator."

The worried face turned back toward Carpenter. After a pause he said, "You're crazy. Does your girl friend here know that you're crazy?"

"How close to Washington?"

"It'll dock at five."

"Good boy. I knew you'd help. I knew you had it in you, Wilby."

The car behind them kept its contact distance. On the turns its lights swept the rear window. The senator and Marvina looked back.

"Are we being followed?" Marvina asked calmly.

"Yes," Carpenter answered.

"Mother of God!" the senator exclaimed, and tucked his head down into his corner as if it were a turtle's returning to its shell.

"Can we do something?" Marvina continued to watch.

"Soon," Carpenter replied. "We have to draw them off some more until their whole net is convinced that we're going in this direction."

"How will you know?"

"When it's time, it'll speed up and try to pass. The two men inside won't want us to get beyond their network, beyond the reach of their people."

"Someone has been back there for a long time."

"Right. Ever since Washington."

Carpenter asked the butler if he could maintain speed, and hold the road if he switched the headlights off.

"I don't know."

"It'll be necessary."

"In that case I'll do it."

Carpenter picked up the rifle from the floor and checked it, set up the other jump seat and moved to it. It was beginning. The pursuing car had sped up.

"Lights off!" Carpenter leaned forward and smashed the rear glass with the barrel. The air rushed in with a flush of whistling and motor sounds. He could make out the outlines of two heads. On the passenger side something was poking through the open window. All he had was surprise. It had to work. First the gunner, then the driver.

The scope on the rifle was of no help. He had to count on quantity. He exploded the entire clip across their windshield.

"Put the lights on," he shouted at the butler.

The car behind them careened sideways, tires screeching. It left the road and pitched down a hill, still upright until it hit a boulder. It was a deafening crash.

"Stop when you can and turn around," he told the butler. "I want to check them out."

He rambled down the hill to the wreck. There hadn't been a good hit. Both men had been grazed, but hunks of glass hung from their faces. The crash had killed them.

The machine gun was in the back seat with its metal

shoulder-stock bent. Loose ammunition clips were strewn all over. He gathered up three and took the gun.

As he climbed back up the hill, he considered the wisdom of continuing in the senator's limousine. The network of surveillance cars had been broken, he decided. There wasn't time enough to be careful now. He had to chance the visibility of an official car.

"Let's find that boatyard," he said to the butler.

Discarding the rifle, he threw the machine gun on the car floor. The senator studied the new weapon at his feet and then Carpenter. "They were going to kill us," he said without emotion.

"I assume that was their intention."

"I don't believe it."

"Don't," Carpenter said.

"You're crazy."

"You said that before. It's been said before you. I'm not. The world's crazy, Wilby, and I'm doing my best to stay alive in it."

"I saw a report on you."

"Just one?"

"You're a paranoid schizophrenic," the senator blurted out.

Carpenter remembered the term. ("You're coming home with me," Fuller had said. "I'll be damned if I'll let them keep you in an institution after those seven years. Paranoid schizophrenic? What the hell do they expect?")

Marvina burbled with laughter. "If he's crazy, so am I," she said.

"You're both crazy. You're not wrong, young woman."

She continued to laugh. "That's fine," she said. "My father and I don't mind being crazy if the rest of you think you're sane."

He felt the warmth he had known earlier. The hostility

he had felt toward Fuller had vanished. He even felt a twinge of sympathy. She had given him something Fuller had always withheld, even as he had given understanding. Always that odd superiority had accompanied it. ("Lessy said it was all right for you to stay with me. He doesn't accept the psychiatric reports. I know why. They're describing him, too." Fuller looked straight into his eyes. "He's not going to let you go, Wes. He needs you to run something he calls MPI. So rest easy. There's always room in Lessy's world for a paranoid like himself.")

Owen.

Fuller's daughter was his daughter now. She understood the dangers of survival. He had taught her.

"There's no excuse for you, miss," the senator whispered. "He at least spent seven years in solitary confinement and had a brave record on behalf of the security of the United States."

"Is that why they're trying to kill him, and me?"

"No one wants to kill anyone."

She was amused by the senator, but suddenly had a flicker of doubt, glancing at Carpenter as if for support.

He took her hand in his and pressed it, hoping that she'd be comforted. Hers were surprisingly cold—tense. He released it when he felt no reciprocal pressure.

"All they're trying to do is capture him for his own good," the senator insisted. "We don't treat heroes by killing them. We weren't able to publicize his achievements because the American people wouldn't understand what must be done to maintain security. And he wouldn't have known the difference anyway."

"What's he talking about?" she asked.

"He doesn't know," Carpenter broke in. "He doesn't understand what they're going to do to him. He was told, but he won't believe it."

He looked out through the jagged hole of the rear window and saw only blackness dotted with streetlights that spun out gloomily over long distances.

"Do we need him?"

The senator pulled back into the corner, trying to disappear. In the dim light of the back seat his face seemed shrunken, afraid again.

"I think so," Carpenter said.

It was uncomfortable to have the drive seem easy. A car had come up behind them, but it hadn't stayed for more than a few miles, and it hadn't been equipped with any obvious communications system. The relief Carpenter felt when it left was replaced with an uneasiness, a feeling that something was wrong. Even the senator had become quiet as if he were expecting sudden rescue.

"It's simple," Carpenter told himself. "We're just not accustomed to the quiet. That has to be it."

When Marvina looked at him, he realized that he had spoken aloud.

"What's simple?"

"We'll be all right," he said. "It's okay. It's an old habit."

Her face showed concern, not acceptance.

"You know me. I get worried when I'm not doing something. There's no reason for us to worry."

The concern didn't fade.

"I expect the worst. The best doesn't happen. It never has. I expect it and so I'm prepared for it."

"I'm not worried," she said, but her face didn't change.

"You always have to be wary," he said. "Lessy is a tricky animal. We can't ever forget that. There's nothing he can't do. We know what he's capable of."

He remembered that it wasn't good to have anger. It was

only useful for motivation; otherwise it dulled reflexes when they were needed.

The senator relaxed from his position; his head and body slumped slightly as he seemed to study Marvina. His hands dropped to his lap and his fingers intertwined.

There was a view of the Potomac, a lazy broad darkness with a long ribbon of lights on the far side. Everyone looked out at it as if trying to see more than what was there. The glowing haze above Washington in the north was indistinct. A large jet went through the center trailing a white funneling tail.

They left the sight of the broad river and drove by the edge of a suburban community with rows of two-story houses studded into lawns and gardens and fences, all bumpy shadows. There were few lights.

"I don't know why you need me on this crazy trip," the senator said.

"You wanted to meet with Lessy, didn't you?"

"Not under these circumstances."

"These are the only ones I'm giving you. Being with me, you might have some luck and make it back to Idaho in one piece."

"In a coffin."

"Anything's possible."

There was another sighting of the river, and once more all three turned to look.

The butler said, "We don't have far to go."

"You're a Goddamned traitor!" Wilby growled.

"Sir?" The butler sounded perplexed.

"Aiding and abetting two murderers! You'll face the same charges!"

The car was silent after the outburst, except for the roar of the engine and the rush of air.

"I'll see to it," the senator added.

"*Shut up*," Marvina cried out.

Wilby saw the determined eyes and returned to his pinched position in the corner.

There was the presidential yacht, standing at anchor in the middle of the river, its fore and aft lights bright. There didn't seem to be any activity aboard. The central deck was ablaze with lights. Nothing moved across them.

CHAPTER EIGHTEEN

The boatyard was closed. A slight mist rose off the edge of the river and crept along every hard surface in sinuous undulations.

Parked, with headlights off, they all watched the mist and the many private boats stretched out into the cove beyond the wooden dock. A single lantern hung on a pole at the far end of the dock. There was a muffled slapping sound as the boats rose and fell in the water.

"There's no one here," the senator pointed out with obvious amusement.

"We'll get somebody," Carpenter said.

"You won't get very far. There'll be Secret Service guarding the President."

"I know. That doesn't worry me, senator."

"I never thought you had a chance."

"You keep thinking that."

Marvina sighed. "Maybe he's right, maybe it's crazy."

"Maybe it is." Carpenter stared along the shoreline before looking at Marvina. "We'll do all right. I wouldn't let him worry you." He stepped out of the limousine, yanking his pistol from his belt. "Okay, senator, I need you with me."

"I'm not going anywhere."

Marvina opened his door, took out her pistol, and aimed it at the center of his stomach.

The senator stared at the weapon and got out. Carpenter ambled around the limousine and grabbed the senator by his arm, pushing him down the path toward the boatyard's dark office. He called back to Marvina to find some cover and to bring the machine gun and ammunition clips. Outside the office, he shoved Wilby forward to the door.

"Make some noise. Tell them that you're a senator of the United States and that you want some attention."

The senator clung to the doorknob and remained silent.

"Make some noise!" Carpenter kicked him in the seat.

The senator yelped, but said nothing. Carpenter leaned past him and hammered on the door, rattling its boards. *"Open up. Wake up. I'm a senator and want some action!"*

A light went on inside the office.

"You start being helpful and act like a senator," Carpenter hissed. He jammed his pistol in the small of Wilby's back. The door opened a chink and a set of eyes peered out.

"Open up," Carpenter demanded. "The senator wants to rent your biggest power boat."

"I'm just a night watchman." A pair of lips appeared beneath the suspicious eyes.

"Get the owner here. Move, man."

"I can't do that."

Carpenter kicked the door open, smacking it against the face.

"Jesus," the night watchman said, staggering back, his hands to his face. The senator leaped inside as Carpenter pushed him hard.

"Call the owner of the yard and tell him that a United States senator wants a boat."

"Yeah? You're kidding me, feller. Where's he from? What's his name?"

"Tell him," Carpenter said.

"My name is Wilby. I'm a senator from Idaho."

"Be fast about it, buddy—the senator has an early morning appointment with the President aboard his yacht. Isn't that right, senator?"

The senator stared with misery at Carpenter and finally turned his attention to the night watchman. He nodded tentatively.

"He didn't hear you, senator."

"That's right."

"I don't know ... it's late at night. I've got my orders."

"Get on the horn. We haven't got this kind of time." The watchman rubbed at his bruised nose. Carpenter brought out his pistol. The watchman looked down at it.

"You're not going to kill someone, are you?" It was a meek question.

"That's not my intention. The senator has a meeting with the President. I wouldn't like him to miss it."

The watchman went to the phone and raised someone after a long minute. "There's a senator here that needs to get out to the President for some kind of meeting. ... Sure I know it's late, but that's what he says." He looked at Carpenter's gun. "I believe him. You bet I believe him. ... I'm sorry I woke you up. I didn't want to rent him a motor launch without getting your say so. Hell, that's what you told me." He turned toward the senator. "He says it's cash on the barrelhead."

"That's no problem," Carpenter said.

"The man says he'll be glad to pay before he takes off. Christ, I don't think he wants it for more than just tonight."

Carpenter nodded.

"He says that's right. ... Sure, I'm positive he's a senator. He's ..."

"Wilby."

"Wilby from—"

"Idaho."

"Senator Wilby from Idaho. Well, isn't that a coincidence?" He smiled at the senator. "He says that he's four-square in back of everything you stand for. He knows all about you." He turned back to the phone. "You bet. I'll let him have the best. Absolutely."

Carpenter fished into his pocket and brought up a handful of crumpled bills. Troubled by the length of the watchman's negotiations, he decided that they had been legitimate, or so they had sounded. He threw the bills on the counter. "That ought to be enough," he said.

The night watchman scuttled behind the counter and began counting.

"Where's the boat?"

The man's attention was on his count.

Marvina entered with a blanket and the butler. "Are we all set?" she asked.

Carpenter nodded and watched the laborious work the night watchman was making of the bills, straightening each, putting it aside, smoothing the pile. It was wrong. Even a slow man would be faster. The senator seemed to know that it was wrong, too: he was smiling. Carpenter nudged the senator forward. "We'll find a launch ourselves," he said.

"I'm not finished." The night watchman smiled.

"I'm not waiting," Carpenter said.

The watchman looked startled. He took a few crab steps to the door as if to halt their progress. Then, glancing at Carpenter, he seemed to change his mind and opened the door. "It looks like enough money," he said and flashed his set of even teeth in friendly compliance.

The teeth disturbed Carpenter. Caps. He was also disturbed by a sudden desire to kill the man, knowing that the internal reflex was a bad sign. He followed the others out onto the dock.

There was the sound of a motor on the Potomac, but nothing could be seen. The sound was distant, an even hum somewhere out on the water.

"You can have that launch there, at the end," the watchman said. "It's a humdinger. Damn it," he said, "I forgot the key." He stopped and began to turn. "I'll be right back."

Carpenter let him go. "We'll go ahead and wait," he said. He and the others continued to the end of the dock, but he didn't board with them. He looked back at the watchman reentering the office, and then he followed.

The older man was on the phone. Carpenter listened from the shadows outside.

"I held them as long as I could. I was surprised to see them at all. I couldn't help it. I did the best I could. This guy is no out-patient."

Carpenter stepped inside and took several long steps and jammed the pistol in the watchman's back. "Tell them it's just the senator and his butler who are coming out."

The watchman's head swiveled. After a moment the head went back to the phone. "They tell me that it's just the senator and his butler who's coming out. . . . That's all I know."

"The other two said they were going to drive to Washington," Carpenter whispered and nudged the old man again.

"The other two told me they were going to drive to Washington. . . . That's all I know. No shit, that's all I know. Listen, this guy is unpredictable."

Carpenter reached in front of the man and hung up for him. "That was very cooperative," he said gratefully. The desire to kill the watchman was gone. Instead he tied him with fishing line after taking the key to the launch. He arranged the line with a loop from the neck to the feet. If the watchman struggled he would strangle himself.

He felt almost joyous as he returned to the dock and

headed toward the lantern at its end and the motor launch.

The senator was standing and gazing over the bow out to the dark river. He turned as Carpenter came aboard. "What are you so damn cheerful about? Are you happy that you're going to get us all killed?"

"What took you so long?" Marvina asked. "Did you have a problem?"

"A minor one."

"Did you shoot him?"

"No. It wasn't necessary."

He went below deck without another word and undid the latch covering the motor. He grinned when he looked at the gray hulk. There was just enough light from the cabin behind to define the surfaces. His eyes followed the thin circuit wiring that emerged from the top and plunged below the motor. Squatting, he groped with his hands until he felt a line of pipelike shapes strapped into a tight package. He ripped it out and drew it into the light, studying it. A red wire dangled free. He felt around again and found a small battery-pack and radio receiver. He took them, too, detaching the radio connection.

When he returned to the deck, he was surprised no one asked what he was carrying. Perhaps it was obvious, he thought. And expected. Then he saw.

"There's a boat on the river," Marvina said. "It's coming closer."

"It's all right," he said. "It won't come too close."

"How do you know?"

"After we start up and this stuff"—he held up the sticks of dynamite—"when this doesn't go up, it'll swing into a circle and transmit to the detonator down there."

"My God!" the senator exclaimed.

The engine of the other boat on the river sounded loud, pervasive, but they could see nothing of it.

"What's the name of our boat?" Carpenter asked.

"*Liz*," the butler answered.

He said aloud to himself, "He wants me to know that he knows. He wants me to think that he planned me to be here." He looked up at the butler. "Do me a favor. Find out if the name has been changed recently."

The senator giggled nervously as Marvina climbed the ladder to join Carpenter at the wheel. She handed him the blanket containing the machine gun and its ammunition. One of the long metal clips fell out and clattered to the deck.

The butler was aft, leaning over the rail.

"Well?" Carpenter said.

The butler straightened and held up a hand. "It's wet, still."

"Is that important?" Marvina asked him quietly.

"Lessy thinks it is." When he discovered that he wasn't moving, that he was standing frozen thinking of the bloated girl in the apartment, he knew Lessy was right.

"You don't have to come with us," he shouted to the butler. "Untie us and push us off."

The butler hesitated, squinting at the senator.

"I'll trust you not to free the night watchman until later."

"Yes, sir. Good luck." The butler climbed from the launch, unhooked the restraining ropes, and pushed the boat from the dock. He stood under the lantern with an arm raised, waving.

Carpenter turned the key and throttled down as soon as the engine caught. The bobbing hull gripped into the black water and heaved forward in a surge.

The motorboat out in the river turned, visible now in its churning wake. The disconnected radio receiver lying on the dashboard in front of Carpenter began clicking.

"We're on our way, kid," he told Marvina.

"I'm not sure," she said.

"There's nothing else we can do. This is the way Lessy

wants it. He didn't think we'd make it this far, but he planned that we might."

"You make it sound like a game."

"It's not a game. It's Lessy. It's the way he thinks."

That didn't explain anything. Fuller might have understood; he always seemed to, but his ideas didn't always make sense. Carpenter had to admit that Fuller was at least partly right. Lessy considered himself superior to everyone.

"We'll make it now," he said to Marvina. "We'll kill the son of a bitch before he gets us. Then we'll be safe." The darkness of the river closed in. "You'll see. Hold this course for me," he told her and stepped aside to make room at the wheel. Picking up the machine gun, he wedged the broken stock into place and crammed a clip into its belly. They were heading upriver toward Washington and the circling power boat had changed its direction to follow.

"When I tell you, make as *hard* a turn as possible and head for the wake of the boat behind us. Hold yourself steady." He looked below him and saw the senator watching the speedboat. "You think they're friends of yours, senator?"

The senator glared up at him.

"You ought to tell them who you are."

Wilby looked back uncertainly.

"Wave to them, senator."

A spotlight suddenly went on from the speedboat. It found the senator.

"Now!"

Marvina twisted the wheel. Shots thudded against the *Liz.*

Carpenter braced himself. The boat fought the turn. As Marvina straightened and headed for the speedboat's wake the other boat was parallel. Carpenter fired the entire clip.

The searchlight stayed lit as the boat twisted away.

"Head up the river," Carpenter said.

Marvina completed the turn and soon had the craft in the middle of the Potomac.

Carpenter looked back as the searchlight sank and went out.

CHAPTER NINETEEN

Carpenter estimated a trip of about thirty minutes before they sighted the presidential yacht. And then there would be a gauntlet of protective craft to run. Darkness wouldn't help because there wouldn't be any. Searchlights and flares were a certainty—part of the reception.

"You don't look optimistic," Marvina said.

He lifted his eyes to see her staring at him. "You think we ought to cut and run?"

"It crossed my mind."

"It's too late. We wouldn't make it. We've got to do it this way now. We always had to. I never told you, but I knew it had to be this way."

"Your eyes are glittering, but the rest of you doesn't tell me the same story."

"How's the senator?" he asked.

She left Carpenter and went to check, descending the ladder.

He could hear them talking, the subdued conversation buried in the smooth roar of the motor and the churning sound of water. He watched the dial in front of him as he slowed, moving closer to shore. It dipped. He wondered if the needle would descend below zero if the craft were in reverse as it might be when maneuvering for a docking. He slowed to a standstill, letting the boat drift.

Marvina appeared at his side. "Why are we stopping?"

He pushed the handle for reverse, the craft skittering as the blades whined and bit. The needle fell below zero. He moved forward again. "What did the senator have to say?"

"Just that you're crazy. He would have jumped overboard long ago, but he doesn't think he could swim to shore and doesn't like the idea of drowning."

"How about you? You want to go overboard?"

"And miss a presidential reception?" she said. "Not on your life preserver."

A glimpse told him that she was smiling. "I hope you can swim," he said.

"You want me to go overboard?"

"We're both going."

"Now?"

"Later. I'm going to let the senator have the boat. He's right, you know."

"About what? I can't imagine that he's right about anything."

"I am crazy."

She didn't speak for a moment. "Just because—"

"No, no. He's right. I've been told that before. Look, Lessy is insane. I knew that. I've been thinking about it. The river is a good place to think. Lessy and I are the same. We believe in the same things. Maybe it's better to say that I accept all he told me. I don't see anything wrong with it, except when he hurt a friend."

"Owen Fuller?"

"Fuller. Yes. That's how it started."

Both had their eyes fixed on the river. She laughed.

"What's funny?"

"If you're crazy, I am, too. I really do think of you as a father. I don't remember what it was like before these last few days. I even found myself thinking that somehow there was a mix-up when I was a baby." She glanced at him. "Were you ever married? Did you have a baby?"

"No."

He reached and touched her, lingering on her cheek with fingertips. They still had some minutes before the yacht came into sight. The glow of the sky and the shoreline lights changed the dark water to a milky patina. Carpenter noticed sailboats and rowboats near the edge.

"I have to make a few preparations," he said. "Can you keep the senator busy for a few minutes? I don't mind if you tell him that you agree with him, that I am crazy."

She nodded and descended the ladder.

With the heel of his hand he gave the speed dial a sharp smack and its plastic cover dropped off. Then he attached one wire of the battery-pack to the needle, hooking the other end to the area below zero, and applied the other in a twist to the dynamite. He stuffed the dynamite under the dash out of sight and broke the tiny lights that lit the dash.

"*Daughter*, I'd like to talk to the senator." He heard them climb up to the wheel. He realized that he had never felt so much tension. His body was rippling with pain. Then he remembered that he had—the time he had attacked his father. Maybe Fuller had been right and he really thought of Lessy and his father as one.

"You wanted to see me?" the senator asked.

"I thought you might be pleased. My daughter and I are going to leave you with the boat."

"Sure you are. They'll blow me out of the water."

"I don't think so. I know Lessy. We'll light you up and put up some flags of surrender. He'll be intrigued. It's your only chance. He planned to kill you. But he'll let you come aboard just to find out about me." He compared the senator's face with the one he had confronted at the hearing. Its arrogance was still there, though reduced by a new overlay of thoughtfulness that resembled a look of wisdom. Carpenter knew it was just fear that had lingered too long.

Wilby assumed an authoritative scowl. "I don't think anyone, least of all Lessy, wanted to kill me." His voice quivered.

"It doesn't matter how you feel, you'll be by yourself. We'll be leaving when we're in sight of the yacht. Your only chance is visibility. There'll be a boarding party. You'll be okay."

"I'd rather be put ashore."

"You don't have that option."

"I see."

Carpenter dismissed him by ignoring him, concentrating his gaze on the river ahead and on the shoreline, spotting another cluster of sailboats. He wondered about the wind direction, if indeed there was any to have direction. He had sailed only once, under different circumstances. The bobbing masts near shore provided no clue. He couldn't make out any pennants.

Marvina said, "I hope we're not dependent on what the senator does."

"What's he doing?"

"He's looking for white flags, hunting through every box on deck."

"That's a good sign."

"He also stops at times and stares at the river as if he's thinking of jumping."

"That can be stopped. Make a tour and find all the life jackets and throw them over the side. There are sleeping quarters below deck. One of the sheets should make a good flag of surrender. But toss all the flotation cushions."

"That'll relieve his mind."

The senator would do as he was told; he had no other option. Lessy was the problem. "The fucking pricks around us are the problem," Lessy had said. "You either pay them off or you catch them with their pants down. Don't risk any other way if you want them to perform." Did Lessy say that? Or had it been his father?

The pain of the tension was like shivering. He flexed his fingers for relief. Movement, action, were all reflex; he couldn't concentrate, his mind cluttered with recurrent pictures of an angry man in a wheelchair, a heavy massive sneering face looming above a bull neck. Then there was the face without eyes. The room, the room with the light and its silence.

"What do you think? Is there someone outside?"

"I don't know. I once thought so. I used to believe that there had to be someone to leave the food in the trap under the door. I'm not sure any more. I think we've been forgotten. There once was someone. He asked questions."

"I remember. Wasn't that a long time ago?"

"I threw the life jackets overboard."

He stared at Marvina. He wondered why he thought of her as his, someone that not only belonged to him, but was his creation, someone part of him. "Good," he said.

He directed the launch toward a far point of land, a turn in the river. The roar of the motor seemed to contain voices, none of which he could understand, but they were frantic, speaking of things he wanted to hear.

"Guard him so that he doesn't jump."

"The senator?"

"He should stay aboard."

"I don't think he will jump."

"We're going close to shore. He might consider it."

She left him again as he throttled down and slowed the boat. He told himself that care was necessary. He had to maintain some forward speed. The engine coughed and barely held while the launch drifted toward a group of sailboats. There was a rowboat among them tied to a buoy. It slapped hard on the water as the wake ran to the shore.

He gunned the motor and pulled out, the launch sliding sideways before nosing toward the center of the river.

As though suddenly awakening, he spun the wheel and ran to the lower deck, leaping down, ignoring the ladder, and reached for the rowboat rope, yanking it loose from the buoy and tying it to the launch in a looping slipknot. Quickly he returned to the wheel. His motions were explosive, instantaneous. The launch thrust forward, back into the current beyond the cove.

"We should see it on the next turn," he said to Marvina, who joined him.

"The little bastard's yacht?"

He grinned. The voice next to him was like the voice within him, saying what he understood.

"I have nothing against the little bastard," he said. "He's not very bright."

"Just Lessy?"

"I think so. I think it's just Lessy." He was confused by her look. She didn't understand that he wasn't sure. Moving ahead at night had its own reasons. Someone was to die. It might as well be Lessy. In the dark it would be hard to tell who. "Lessy," he said. "Of course, Lessy. Forgive me, I don't give it much thought when my assignment comes to this point."

"Assignment?"

"I don't mean assignment. Objective, that's the word."

He was in the main channel of the Potomac. There was a spit of land bumping out into the next bend. He listened to the rowboat scraping the side of the launch in a moaning shriek as he let speed be his entire consideration, opening out the engine, feeling the front lift up and the propeller dig into the water with a deep growl. The boat shuddered.

"It won't be long," he said.

"I'm scared," she said.

"I always am." That wasn't true. Inside, there was sometimes a voice that said it was scared and never seemed content unless he agreed. ("You Goddamn pricks, when I'm done with you, you'll forget that you think. You'll act like I tell you to act. Every fucking thing I say, you do. There is nothing but what I fucking say.")

He gestured to Marvina that he wanted her to take the wheel. "Keep her wide open until we get around the bend."

"What are you going to do?"

He didn't answer. He didn't know. His body tensed. He went below, grabbing the machine gun and its ammunition, startling the senator who stood holding a white sheet.

"*You're crazy*," the senator shouted. "This won't work! They'll blow me out of the water!"

He leaned over the side and lowered the machine gun into the bottom of the rowboat and dropped two clips with it; they skittered along the wooden bottom. He stared into the rowboat, and then turned to the senator. "It won't be long," he said. "We'll find out."

His face damp from the spray, he watched the area ahead as they cleared the bend, and squinted at the sight of the broad river with the yacht in the middle. There was a wide wash of light like an inverted bowl, covering the area around the yacht. Searchlights probed beyond.

"Father!" Marvina called as she saw two speedboats hustle from the vicinity of the large anchored yacht and come bouncing toward them.

"Take over, senator, it's all yours. Good luck."

The sheet unfurled as the senator dashed forward and climbed the ladder. The sheet was like an enormous banner. Wilby held it in one hand while trying to control the launch with the other.

Carpenter kicked his shoes off and undressed quickly,

throwing his jacket and pants and pistol into the rowboat. Marvina took only a moment before following his example, not even embarrassed by the absence of a bra.

"It'll be cold," he said, and freed the rowboat. Then he leaped far out into the river, vaguely aware that she was behind him.

CHAPTER TWENTY

"Where are we going?" Marvina asked. She held to the edge of the rowboat on the dark shore side as he floated behind, swimming with it as it bobbed violently.

"Ssh."

She fell silent as the small boat slowly settled into the decreasing swells and finally was caught in a shore eddy that moved it toward the edge of the river. A star shell rose into the air above, its burning track hot and straight. It burst high above and night was gone.

There was the senator holding aloft a long sheet. A speedboat was alongside and two figures were boarding the launch. The senator's voice could be heard above the idling motor as he screamed, "I'm by myself! I'm by myself! Carpenter's not here! I demand to see Mr. Lessy! I'm a friend of his! He'll want to see me! For God's sake, don't kill me!"

The panic in his voice filled the Potomac stillness.

One of the figures moved with the senator down to the deck below while the other took the wheel. The white sheet sailed free a moment, came down on the river, and disappeared.

Carpenter pushed the rowboat toward the nearby sailboats and then among them. He pulled himself aboard and felt along the bottom until he found the machine gun and the clips.

He spoke in a mumble. "I want you to untie one of the sailboats and paddle it out this way. When you're close, get in it and stay down. They'll be coming soon to try to find us. Don't worry."

"What's happening?"

"I can't tell yet. The senator and his new friends are going in slow circles at the moment."

Another illumination flare went up from the deck of the yacht and the shadows vanished again as it blossomed overhead. The thin burning track collapsed in a dead curve.

Marvina slithered aboard the sailboat. Carpenter handed her the clothes and weapons, except the machine gun. He loaded it and stood in the bright light. The distance to the yacht was impossible. He wouldn't do more than attract attention. The launch continued its lazy circle. He could see the senator standing alone, the figure with him climbing up into the wheel housing. Another speedboat idled next to the launch. The senator pointed in Carpenter's direction and the companion boat suddenly dug into the water, throttle open, and spun about, skipping as if on a cushion of air.

The decks of the presidential yacht came alive with people. An entertainment was about to be staged, the audience was gathering. Several people on the afterdeck were pointing toward Carpenter.

He was suddenly weary, the tightness gone. He slumped on the rowboat seat listlessly awaiting the end.

"Can you see what's happening?" Marvina asked from the crater of the sailboat.

"There's nothing to do until they get here," he said.

She sat up, shimmering in the light, her white skin oily from the water.

A spotlight from the yacht fell on them like an additional indignity.

"What happened?"

"It didn't . . . the distance. I didn't expect it to be so

great. There's something else wrong. There's no wind."

"For the sailboat?"

"It wouldn't have helped. We're not close enough."

The senator was waving to those on the yacht. He looked triumphant.

"Will they kill us?"

"I'm sorry," he said. He shut his eyes to close off her look of condemnation and wondered where his anger had gone, his desire. There were no images in his head, only the light. Why didn't they turn off the light? It had been burning within its cage . . . for how long. How did they manage to change it when it was exhausted? It never went out. It never allowed him to think or sleep. Had he ever slept, he wondered. There were times when he remembered nothing but the burning in his eyes.

"We can't stay here," she said.

He opened his eyes in the blinding brightness. It took a moment to focus on her. Another shell burst open in the sky and the shadows disappeared again. He looked out over the river. Two speedboats drew closer. The launch was edging to the yacht and the senator was readying himself to jump to a stair platform standing ready at the side. A sailor had a hand out to help.

How long would he be there under the light? The scene of the jubilant senator leaping aboard the yacht was without sense. It was smeared at its core with whiteness.

Marvina was screaming. He looked at her. He didn't understand, neither her words nor her gestures. She was standing and pumping her arms excitedly. There was a roaring sound that drowned her out. He turned to see what she wanted him to see.

The speedboats were no longer coming. They were spinning crazily.

The light in the sky was slowly dying, but there was still brightness. The entire river seemed lit, burning with an internal fire. The noise was unbearable, louder than he could imagine it to be. He thought he heard voices within it, like whispers.

The water was burning. The center of the Potomac was fire.

"*My God!*" Marvina shouted. "*My God!*"

He thought that it was nice that his daughter was so surprised.

"We *made* it! You've done it! You saved us!" she continued to shriek happily.

He wished she weren't far away from him and that they could return to another time when she was little. He didn't remember her as just a little girl. All of that was gone as if it had never happened. All he saw was his daughter, grown up now. He wanted to begin all over again, desperately. He would remember this time and never forget.

"Look!" Marvina called, a finger pointed out into the river.

The flame on the water was swarming over a large boat that was slowly sinking. Bright shining figures were leaping into the fire and disappearing like dead sparks. The river was glistening with black slick just before a final explosion and a last burst of flame as the yacht vanished. Anguished cries reached them over the sound of the fire. Then silence. The light decreased.

He was tired, feeling as if life itself were ebbing away. He dropped the heavy metal object he had been clutching. He didn't know what it was. He didn't care. He no longer had the strength.

"It's all over," Marvina said.

He nodded, not knowing what she meant, disappointed that his daughter seemed unhappy that the fireworks had ended. It was strange, he thought. He loved her so much and could remember so little of her.

It was becoming so dark.

CHAPTER TWENTY-ONE

He wondered why the lights never seemed to go out. At least there were people in the small room, but nothing they said made sense. They were all familiar, but he was certain only of his daughter. She was there all the time.

"I don't think he understands much," his daughter said.

"Try. He seems to listen to you."

"Father, this is Senator Dobentz and his committee counsel, William Roose. You met them a month ago when you testified. Try to remember. It's very important."

He blinked his eyes and closed them. He liked hearing her voice; he wished he understood. She seemed to want him to understand, her face showed so much effort. He wondered what she was doing in Indochina.

"You can see how difficult it is," she said.

"Does he know that Roland Lessy is dead?"

"I don't think so. I'm convinced he hears me but that's all."

"Isn't it ironic that he doesn't know what he did?"

"He wouldn't have known anyway," she said.

"It doesn't matter. We wouldn't make it a public announcement. Americans aren't really prepared to know either. If Carpenter didn't understand, why would anyone else?"

"He might have, in time," she said. "I didn't then either. All we wanted to do was stay alive."

"Amazing."

"It's not, really. My father was a very well-trained agent. Roland Lessy can take credit for him. But he never understood that somewhere in each human there's a strange spark that ignites. You never know what lights it."

"Why do you call him your father? He's not, is he?"

"Oh God, yes. I don't know why, but I know he is. If there's nothing else I understand, it's that Wesley Carpenter is my father. I know it's crazy, but I know that's true."

How long has it been, he wondered. Long. This was a different cell. Strange. He didn't know how they had moved him or how they changed the ever-burning light, but it was different. Now he wasn't entirely alone. Somehow his daughter was there. She always seemed to be there.

Lawrence Kamarck is the author of *The Dinosaur*, for which he won the Edgar Allan Poe Special Award in 1969, and *The Bellringer*. His third novel was *The Zinsser Implant*.

A former reporter for *Newsweek* and *Forbes* magazines, Mr. Kamarck and his family now live in New Hampshire.